Also by Sara Paretsky

A V I WARSHAWSKI NOVEL

SARA PARETSKY

TOTAL RECALL

DELACORTE PRESS

Published by
DELACORTE PRESS
Random House, Inc.
1540 Broadway
New York, New York 10036

The notebook entries on pages 165, 169, 307 and 308 are set
in Sütterlin, a font created by Waldenfont.com that replicates
the handwriting script taught in German schools at the time.

Delacorte Press® is a registered trademark
of Random House, Inc.,
and the colophon is a trademark of
Random House, Inc.

ISBN 0-385-31366-7

Manufactured in the United States of America
Published simultaneously in Canada

For Sara Krupnik and Hannah Paretsky,
whose names I bear

May the One who establishes
peace in the high places
grant us all peace

Thanks

Thanks to Wolfson College, Oxford, where I was a Visiting Scholar in 1997, which enabled me to pursue archival research. Thanks to Dr. Jeremy Black of Wolfson for making my time there possible.

The archives of letters and audiotapes in the Imperial War Museum, London, are an important source about the Kindertransport, England's generous acceptance of ten thousand Jewish children from central Europe in the years immediately before the Second World War. As is true of librarians everywhere, those at the Imperial War Museum were extremely helpful—even allowing me into the archives on a day they were closed when I confused an appointment date.

The Royal Free Hospital, London, gave me access to their archives, allowed me to send Lotty Herschel to school there, and were in general most helpful.

Dr. Dulcie Reed, Dr. Lettice Bowen, Dr. Peter Scheuer, and Dr. Judith Levy, all of whom trained in medicine in Great Britain around the same time as Lotty Herschel, were generous in giving me time and information about that period in their lives.

In the case of all archival material, as well as the reminiscences of these four doctors, I have avoided turning people's real-life experiences into fiction—with the exception of Lotty and her roommates making lingerie out of parachute silk: Dr. Bowen and her friends did this—an amazing feat, as anyone who has ever tried to construct lingerie from scratch will appreciate.

Professor Colin Divall of the Institute of Railway Studies, York, was helpful with information about train routes and timetables in the 1940's.

Because of the constraints of a novel focusing on Chicago, contemporary crime, and V I Warshawski, I was not able to make as deep a use of any of my English research as I would have wished; perhaps it will find a home in a different story on another day.

In Chicago, Kimball Wright advised me on the guns used in the book. Forensic pathologist Dr. Robert Kirschner was helpful in making accurate the deaths and near deaths of various unfortunate characters; the events described in Chapters 38 and 43 do happen. Sandy Weiss was helpful as always on forensic engineering arcana.

Jolynn Parker did invaluable research on a number of topics, including finding street maps of Jewish neighborhoods of Vienna in the 1930's. More important, her astuteness as a reader helped me pick my way through some thorny problems as I developed the story line. Jonathan Paretsky helped with German, Yiddish—and star-gazing.

Special thanks to Kate Jones for her insightful discussion of this novel, both at its end and at its beginnings.

As always, the first C-dog was there with advice, encouragement—and renewable kneecaps.

This is a work of fiction. No resemblance is intended between any character in this novel and any real person, living or dead, whether in public office, in corporate boardrooms, on the streets, or in any other walk of life. Similarly, all the institutions involved, including Ajax Insurance, Edelweiss Re, Gargette et Cie, are phantasms of the author's fevered brain and are not intended to resemble any actual existing body. The issues of slave reparations and Holocaust asset recovery are very real; the positions taken on them by characters in the novel do not necessarily reflect the author's own, nor should they be taken to reflect the positions taken by people in public life who are debating them.

Note: Anna Freud's "An Experiment in Group Upbringing" is in Volume IV of her collected works. The adult lives of the children she describes are explored in Sarah Moskovitz's *Love Despite Hate*.

Contents

TOTAL RECALL

Lotty Herschel's Story:

Work Ethic

The cold that winter ate into our bones. You can't imagine, living where you turn a dial and as much heat as you want glows from the radiator, but everything in England then was fueled by coal and there were terrible shortages the second winter after the war. Like everyone I had little piles of six-penny bits for the electric fire in my room, but even if I'd been able to afford to run it all night it didn't provide much warmth.

One of the women in my lodgings got a length of parachute silk from her brother, who'd been in the RAF. We all made camisoles and knickers out of it. We all knew how to knit back then; I unraveled old sweaters to make scarves and vests—new wool cost a fortune.

We saw newsreels of American ships and planes bringing the Germans whatever they needed. While we swathed ourselves in blankets and sweaters and ate grey bread with butter substitutes, we joked bitterly that we'd done the wrong thing, bringing the Americans in to win the war— they'd treat us better if we'd lost, the same woman who'd gotten the parachute silk said.

Of course, I had started my medical training, so I couldn't spend much time wrapped up in bed. Anyway, I was glad to have the hospital to go to—although the wards weren't warm, either: patients and sisters would huddle around the big stove in the center of the ward, drinking tea and telling stories—we students used to envy their camaraderie. The sisters expected us medical students to behave professionally—frankly, they enjoyed ordering us about. We'd do rounds with two pairs of tights on, hoping the consultants wouldn't notice we wore gloves as we trailed after them from bed to bed, listening to symptoms that came from deprivation as much as anything.

Working sixteen or eighteen hours a day without proper food took a toll on all of us. Many of my fellow students succumbed to tuberculosis and were granted leave—the only reason the hospital would let you interrupt your training and come back, as a matter of fact, even though some took more than a year to recover. The new antibiotics were starting to come in, but they cost the earth and weren't yet widely available. When my turn came and I went to the Registrar, explaining that a family friend had a cottage in Somerset where I could recuperate, she nodded bleakly: we were already down five in my class, but she signed the forms for me and told me to write monthly. She stressed that she would hope to see me in under a year.

In fact, I was gone eight months. I'd wanted to return sooner, but Claire—Claire Tallmadge, who was a senior houseman by then, with a consultancy all but certain—persuaded me I wasn't strong enough, although I was aching to get back.

When I returned to the Royal Free it felt—oh, so good. The hospital routine, my studies, they were like a balm, healing me. The Registrar actually called me into her office to warn me to slow down; they didn't want me to suffer a relapse.

She didn't understand that work was my only salvation. I suppose it had already become my second skin. It's a narcotic, the oblivion overwork can bring you. *Arbeit macht frei*—that was an obscene parody the Nazis thought up, but it is possible *Arbeit macht betäubt*—what? Oh, sorry, I forgot you don't speak German. They had 1984-type slogans over the entrance to all their camps, and that was what they put over Auschwitz: *work will make you free*. That slogan was a bestial parody, but work can numb you. If you stop working even for a moment, everything inside you starts evaporating; soon you are so shapeless you can't move at all. At least, that was my fear.

When I first heard about my family, I became utterly without any grounding at all. I was supposed to be preparing for my higher-school certificate—the diploma we took in those days when we finished high school—the results determined your university entrance—but the exams lost the meaning they'd had for me all during the war. Every time I sat down to read I felt as though my insides were being sucked away by a giant vacuum cleaner.

In a perverse way, cousin Minna came to my rescue. Ever since I arrived on her doorstep she had been unsparing in her criticisms of my mother. The news of my mother's death brought not even a respectful silence but a greater barrage. I can see now, through the prism of experience, that guilt drove her as much as anything: she had hated my mother, been jealous of her for so many years, she couldn't admit now that she'd been unfeeling, even cruel. She was probably grief-stricken as well, because her own mother had also perished, all that family that used to spend summers talking and swimming at Kleinsee; well, never mind that. It's old news now.

I would come home from walking the streets, walking until I was too exhausted to feel anything, to Minna: you think you're suffering? That you're the only person who was ever orphaned, left alone in a strange country? And weren't you supposed to give Victor his tea? He says he waited for over an hour for you and finally had to make it himself because you're too much a lady—*"meine gnädige Dame"*—Minna only ever spoke German at home—she had never really mastered English, which made her furious with shame—and she curtsied to me—to get your hands dirty doing work, housework or a real job. You're just like Lingerl. I wonder how a princess like her lived as long as she did in such a setting, with no one to pamper her. Did she tilt her head and bat her eyes so that the guards or other inmates gave up their bread to her? Madame Butterfly is dead. It's time you learned what real work is.

A fury rose up in me greater than any I remember since. I smacked her in the mouth and screamed, if people took care of my mother it's because she repaid them with love. And if they don't care for you it's because you're utterly loathsome.

She stared at me for a moment, her mouth slack with shock. She recovered quickly, though, and hit me back so hard she split my lip with her big ring. And then hissed, the only reason I let a mongrel like you accept that scholarship to the comprehensive was on the understanding that you would repay my generosity by taking care of Victor. Which I might point out you have failed utterly to do. Instead of giving him tea you've been flaunting yourself at the pubs and dance halls just like your mother. Max or Carl or one of those other immigrant boys is likely to give you the same present that Martin, as he liked to call himself, gave Madame Butterfly. Tomorrow morning I'm off to that precious headmistress, that Miss Skeffing you're so fond of, to tell her you can't continue your education. It's time you started pulling your weight around here.

Blood pouring down my face, I ran pell-mell across London to the youth hostel where my friends lived—you know, Max and Carl and the rest of them: when they turned sixteen the year before they hadn't been able to stay in their foster homes. I begged them to find me a bed for the night. In the morning, when I knew Minna would be with her great love, the glove factory, I sneaked back for my books and my clothes—it was only two changes of underwear and a second dress. Victor was dozing in the living room, but he didn't wake up enough to try to stop me.

Miss Skeffing found a family in North London who gave me a room in exchange for doing their cooking. And I began to study as if my mother's life could be redeemed by my work. As soon as I finished the supper dishes I would solve chemistry and math problems, sometimes sleeping only four hours until it was time to make the family's morning tea. And after that, I never stopped working, really.

That was where the story ended, sitting on a hillside on a dull October day overlooking a desolate landscape, listening to Lotty until she could talk no more. It's harder for me to figure out where it began.

Looking back now, now that I'm calm, now that I can think, it's still hard to say, Oh, it was because of this, or because of that. It was a time when I had a million other things on my mind. Morrell was getting ready to leave for Afghanistan. I was worrying most about that, but of course I was trying to run my business, and juggle the nonprofit work I do, and pay my bills. I suppose my own involvement began with Isaiah Sommers, or maybe the Birnbaum Foundation conference—they happened on the same day.

I

Baby-Sitters' Club

They wouldn't even start the funeral service. The church was full, ladies were crying. My uncle was a deacon and he was a righteous man, he'd been a member of that church for forty-seven years when he passed. My aunt was in a state of total collapse, as you can imagine. And for them to have the nerve to say the policy had already been cashed in. When! That's what I want to know, Ms. Warashki, when was it ever cashed in, with my uncle paying his five dollars a week for fifteen years like he did, and my aunt never hearing word one of him borrowing against the policy or converting it."

Isaiah Sommers was a short, square man who spoke in slow cadences as if he were himself a deacon. It was an effort to keep from drowsing off during the pauses in his delivery. We were in the living room of his South Side bungalow, at a few minutes after six on a day that had stretched on far too long already.

I'd been in my office at 8:30, starting a round of the routine searches that make up the bulk of my business, when Lotty Herschel called with an SOS. "You know Max's son brought Calia and Agnes with him from London, don't you? Agnes suddenly has a chance to show her slides at a Huron Street gallery, but she needs a minder for Calia."

"I'm not a baby-sitter, Lotty," I'd said impatiently; Calia was Max Loewenthal's five-year-old granddaughter.

Lotty swept imperiously past that protest. "Max called me when they couldn't find anyone—it's his housekeeper's day off. He's going to that conference at the Hotel Pleiades, although I've told him many times that all he's doing is exposing—but that's neither here nor there. At any rate, he's on a panel at ten—otherwise he'd stay home himself. I tried Mrs. Coltrain at my clinic, but everyone's tied up. Michael is rehearsing all afternoon with the symphony and this could be an important chance for Agnes. Vic—I realize it's an imposition, but it would be only for a few hours."

"Why not Carl Tisov?" I asked. "Isn't he staying at Max's, too?"

"Carl as a baby-sitter? Once he picks up his clarinet the roof of the house can blow off without his noticing. I saw it happen once, during the V-1 raids. Can you tell me yes or no? I'm in the middle of surgical rounds, and I have a full schedule at the clinic." Lotty is the chief perinatologist at Beth Israel.

I tried a few of my own connections, including my part-time assistant who has three foster children, but no one could help out. I finally agreed with a surly lack of grace. "I have a client meeting at six on the far South Side, so someone had better be able to step in before five."

When I drove up to Max's Evanston home to collect Calia, Agnes Loewenthal was breathlessly grateful. "I can't even find my slides. Calia was playing with them and stuck them in Michael's cello, which got him terribly cross, and now the wretched beast can't imagine where he's flung them."

Michael appeared in a T-shirt with his cello bow in one hand. "Darling, I'm sorry, but they have to be in the drawing room—that's where I was practicing. Vic, I can't thank you enough—can we take you and Morrell to dinner after our Sunday afternoon concert?"

"We can't do that, Michael!" Agnes snapped. "That's Max's dinner party for Carl and you."

Michael played cello with the Cellini Chamber Ensemble, the London group started back in the forties by Max and Lotty's friend Carl Tisov. The Cellini was in Chicago to kick off their biannual international tour. Michael was also scheduled to play some concerts with the Chicago Symphony.

Agnes gave Calia a quick hug. "Victoria, thank you a million times. Please, though, no television. She only gets an hour a week and I don't think American shows are suitable for her." She darted back into the drawing room, where we could hear her furiously tossing cushions from the couch. Calia grimaced and clutched my hand.

It was Max who actually got Calia into her jacket and saw that her dog, her doll, and her "favoritest story" were in her day pack. "So much chaos," he grunted. "You'd think they were trying to launch the space shuttle, wouldn't you. Lotty tells me you have an evening appointment on the South Side. Perhaps you could meet me in the Pleiades lobby at four-thirty. I should be able to finish up by then so I can collect this whirling dervish from you. If you have a crisis, my secretary will be able to reach me. Victoria, we are grateful." He walked outside with us, kissing Calia lightly on the head and me on the hand.

"I hope your panel isn't too painful an outing," I said.

He smiled. "Lotty's fears? She's allergic to the past. I don't like wallowing in it, but I think it can be healthy for people to understand it."

I strapped Calia into the backseat of the Mustang. The Birnbaum Foundation, which often underwrites communications issues, had decided to hold a conference on "Christians and Jews: a New Millennium, a New Dialogue." They came up with the program after Southern Baptists announced plans to send a hundred thousand missionaries to Chicago this past summer to convert the Jews. The Baptist drive fizzled out; only about a thousand stalwart evangelizers showed up. It cost the Baptists something in cancelation fees at the hotels, too, but by then the planning for the Birnbaum conference was well under way.

Max was taking part in the bank-account panel, which infuriated Lotty: he was going to describe his postwar experiences in trying to track down his relatives and their assets. Lotty said he was going to expose his misery for the world at large to stare at. She said it only reinforced a stereotype of Jews as victims. Besides, she would add, dwelling on missing assets only gave people fuel for the second popular stereotype, that all Jews cared about was money. To which Max invariably replied, Who cares about money here, really? The Jews? Or the Swiss who refuse to return it to the people who earned it and deposited it? And the fight went on from there. It had been an exhausting summer, being around them.

In the seat behind me, Calia was chattering happily. The private eye as baby-sitter: it wasn't the first image you got from pulp fiction. I don't think Race Williams or Philip Marlowe ever did baby-sitting, but by the end of the morning I decided that was because they were too weak to take on a five-year-old.

I started at the zoo, thinking trudging around for an hour would make Calia eager to rest while I did some work in my office, but that proved to be an optimism born of ignorance. She colored for ten minutes, needed to go to the bathroom, wanted to call

Grandpapa, thought we should play tag in the hall that runs the length of the warehouse where I lease space, was "terrifically" hungry despite the sandwiches we'd eaten at the zoo, and finally jammed one of my picklocks into the back of the photocopier.

At that point I gave up and took her to my apartment, where the dogs and my downstairs neighbor gave me a merciful respite. Mr. Contreras, a retired machinist, was delighted to let her ride horseback on him in the garden. The dogs joined in. I left them to it while I went up to the third floor to make some calls. I sat at the kitchen table with the back door open so I could keep an ear cocked for when Mr. Contreras's patience waned, but I did manage to get an hour of work in. After that Calia consented to sit in my living room with Peppy and Mitch while I read her "favoritest" story, *The Faithful Dog and the Princess.*

"I have a dog, too, Aunt Vicory," she announced, pulling a blue stuffed one from her day pack. "His name is Ninshubur, like in the book. See, it says, *Ninshubur means 'faithful friend' in the language of the princess's people.*"

"Vicory" was the closest Calia could get to Victoria when we met almost three years ago. We'd both been stuck with it ever since.

Calia couldn't read yet, but she knew the story by heart, chanting "For far rather would I die than lose my liberty" when the princess flung herself into a waterfall to escape an evil enchantress. "Then Ninshubur, the faithful hound, leapt from rock to rock, heedless of any danger." He jumped into the river and carried the princess to safety.

Calia pushed her blue plush dog deep into the book, then threw him on the floor to demonstrate his leap into the waterfall. Peppy, well-bred golden retriever that she was, sat on the alert, waiting for a command to fetch, but her son immediately bounded after the toy. Calia screamed, running after Mitch. Both dogs began to bark. By the time I rescued Ninshubur, all of us were on the brink of tears. "I hate Mitch, he is a bad dog, I am most annoyed at his behavior," Calia announced.

I was thankful to see that it was three-thirty. Despite Agnes's prohibition, I plunked Calia in front of the television while I went down the hall to shower and change. Even in the era of casual dress, new clients respond better to professionalism: I put on a sage rayon suit with a rose silk sweater.

When I got back to the living room, Calia was lying with her head on Mitch's back, blue Ninshubur between his paws. She bitterly resisted restoring Mitch and Peppy to Mr. Contreras.

"Mitch will miss me, he will cry," she wailed, so tired herself that nothing made sense to her.

"Tell you what, baby: we'll get Mitch to give Ninshubur one of his dog tags. That way Ninshubur will remember Mitch when he can't see him." I went into my storage closet, where I found one of the small collars we'd used when Mitch had been a puppy. Calia stopped crying long enough to help buckle it in place around Ninshubur. I attached a set of Peppy's old tags, which looked absurdly big on the small blue neck but brought Calia enormous satisfaction.

I stuffed her day pack and Ninshubur into my own briefcase and scooped her up to carry her to my car. "I'm not a baby, I don't get carried," she sobbed, clinging to me. In the car she fell asleep almost at once.

My plan had been to leave my car with the Pleiades Hotel valet for fifteen minutes while I took Calia in to find Max, but when I pulled off Lake Shore Drive at Wacker, I saw this wasn't going to be possible. A major crowd was blocking the entrance to the Pleiades driveway. I craned my head, trying to see. A demonstration, apparently, with pickets and bullhorns. Television crews added to the chaos. Cops were furiously whistling cars away, but the traffic was so snarled I had to sit for some minutes in mounting frustration, wondering where I would find Max and what to do with Calia, heavily asleep behind me.

I pulled my cell phone out of my briefcase, but the battery was dead. And I couldn't find the in-car charger. Of course not: I'd left it in Morrell's car when he and I went to the country for a day last week. I pounded the steering wheel in useless frustration.

As I sat fuming, I watched the picketers, who belonged to conflicting causes. One group, all white, was carrying signs demanding passage of the Illinois Holocaust Asset Recovery Act. "No deals with thieves," they were chanting, and "Banks, insurers, where is our money?"

The man with the bullhorn was Joseph Posner. He'd been on the news so many times lately I could have picked him out in a bigger crowd than this. He was dressed in the long coat and bowler hat of the ultra-Orthodox. The son of a Holocaust survivor, he had become ostentatiously religious in a way that made Lotty grind her teeth. He could be seen picketing everything from X-rated movies, with the support of Christian fundamentalists, to Jewish-owned stores like Neiman Marcus that were open on Saturday. His followers, who seemed to be a cross between a yeshiva and the Jewish

Defense League, accompanied him everywhere. They called themselves the Maccabees and seemed to think their protests should be modeled on the original Maccabees' military prowess. Like a growing number of fanatics in America, they were proud of their arrest records.

Posner's most recent cause was an effort to get Illinois to pass the Illinois Holocaust Asset Recovery Act. The IHARA, suggested by legislation in Florida and California, would bar insurance companies from doing business in the state unless they proved that they weren't sitting on any life or property claims from Holocaust victims. It also had clauses dealing with banks and with firms that benefited from use of forced labor during the Second World War. Posner had been able to generate enough publicity that the bill was being debated in committee.

The second group outside the Pleiades, mostly black, was carrying signs with a large red slash through *Pass the IHARA*. NO DEALS WITH SLAVE OWNERS and ECONOMIC JUSTICE FOR ALL, their signs proclaimed. The guy leading this group was also easy to recognize: Alderman Louis "Bull" Durham. Durham had been looking for a long time for a cause that would turn him into a high-profile opponent to the mayor, but opposition to the IHARA didn't strike me as a citywide issue.

If Posner had his Maccabees, Durham had his own militant followers. He'd set up Empower Youth Energy teams, first in his own ward and then around town, as a way of getting young men off the streets and into job-training programs. But some of the EYE teams, as they were called, had a shadier side. There were whispers on the street of extortion and beatings for store owners who didn't contribute to the alderman's political campaigns. And Durham himself always had his own group of EYE-team bodyguards, who surrounded him in their signature navy blazers whenever he appeared in public. If the Maccabees and the EYE team were going head to head, I was glad I was a private detective trying to make my way through traffic, not one of the policemen hoping to keep them apart.

The traffic finally inched me past the hotel entrance. I turned east onto Randolph Street, where it perches over Grant Park. All the meters there were taken, but I figured the cops were too busy at the Pleiades to spare time for ticketing.

I locked my briefcase in the trunk and pulled Calia from the backseat. She woke briefly, then slumped against my shoulder. She wasn't going to manage the walk to the hotel. I gritted my teeth. Making the best load I could of her forty-pound deadweight, I staggered down the stairs leading to the lower level of Columbus Drive, where the hotel's service entrance lay. It was already almost five: I hoped I'd find Max without too much trouble.

As I'd hoped, no one was blocking the lower entrance. I walked past the attendants with Calia and rode the elevator up to the lobby level. The crowd here was as thick as the mob outside, if quieter. Hotel guests and Birnbaum conference participants were wedged around the doors, anxiously wondering what was going on and what to do about it.

I was despairing of finding Max in this mob when I spotted a face I knew: Al Judson, the Pleiades security chief, was near the revolving doors, talking on a two-way radio.

I elbowed my way to him. "What's up, Al?"

Judson was a small black man, unobtrusive in crowds, an ex-cop who'd learned how to keep an eye on volatile groups from patrolling Grant Park with my dad forty years ago. When he saw me he gave a smile of genuine pleasure. "Vic! Which side of the door are you here for?"

I laughed, but with some embarrassment: my dad and I had argued about my joining antiwar protesters in Grant Park when he was assigned to riot control duty. I'd been a teenager with a dying mother and emotions so tangled I hadn't known what I wanted. So I'd run wild with the Yippies for a night.

"I need to find this small person's grandfather. Should I take to the streets instead?"

"Then you'd have to choose between Durham and Posner."

"I know about Posner's crusade on the life-insurance payments, but what's Durham's?"

Judson hunched a shoulder. "He wants the state to make it illegal for a company to do business here if they profited from slavery in the U.S. Unless they pay restitution to the descendants of slaves, that is. So he says, Don't pass the IHARA unless you add that clause to it."

I gave a little whistle of respect: the Chicago City Council had passed a resolution demanding reparations for descendants of slaves. Resolutions are a nice gesture—nods to constituencies without costing businesses anything. The mayor might be in an awkward spot if he fought Durham publicly over turning the resolution into a law with teeth in it.

It was an interesting political problem, but not as immediate a one for me as Calia, who was making my arms feel as though they were on fire. One of Judson's subordinates was hovering, ready to snatch his attention. I quickly explained my need to find Max. Judson spoke into his lapel radio. Within a few minutes, a young woman from hotel security appeared with Max, who took Calia from me. She stirred and began to cry. He and I had time for a few flustered words, about his panel, the melee outside, Calia's day, before I left him the unenviable task of soothing Calia and getting her to his car.

As I sat in the thicket of traffic waiting to move back past the protest site toward Lake Shore Drive, I nodded off several times. By the time I reached Isaiah Sommers's house in Avalon Park, I was thick with sleepiness. I was almost twenty minutes late, though. He swallowed his annoyance as best he could, but it wouldn't do for me to fall asleep in front of him.

II

Cash on the Coffin

When did your aunt give the policy to the funeral home?" I shifted on the couch, the heavy plastic covering the upholstery crinkling as I moved.

"On the Wednesday. My uncle passed on the Tuesday. They came for the body in the morning, but before they would collect it, they wanted proof that she could pay for the funeral. Which was scheduled for the Saturday. My mother had gone over to be with my aunt, and she found the policy in Uncle Aaron's papers just like we knew it would be. He was methodical in everything he did, great and small, and he was methodical in his documents, as well."

Sommers massaged his neck with his square hands. He was a lathe operator for the Docherty Engineering Works; his neck and shoulder muscles were bunched from leaning over a machine every day. "Then, like I said, when my aunt got to the church on Saturday they told her they weren't starting the funeral until she came up with the money."

"So after they took your uncle's body on Wednesday, the funeral parlor must have called the policy number in to the company, who told them that the policy had already been cashed. What a horrible experience for all of you. Did the funeral director know who the money had been paid to?"

"That's just my point." Sommers pounded his fist on his knee.

"They said it was to my aunt. And that they wouldn't do the funeral—well, I told you all that."

"So how did you manage to get your uncle buried? Or did you?" I had an uneasy vision of Aaron Sommers lying in cold storage until the family shelled out three thousand dollars.

"I came up with the money." Isaiah Sommers looked reflexively toward the hall: his wife, who had let me in, had made clear her disapproval of his exerting himself for his uncle's widow. "And believe me, it wasn't so easy. If you're worried about your fee, don't be: I can take care of that. And if you can find out who took the money, maybe we can get it back. We'd even give you a finder's fee. The policy was worth ten thousand dollars."

"I don't need a finder's fee, but I will need to see the policy."

He lifted a presentation copy of *Roots* from the coffee table. The policy was folded carefully underneath.

"Do you have a photocopy of it?" I asked. "No? I'll mail you one tomorrow. You know that my fee is a hundred dollars an hour, with a minimum of five hours' work, right? I charge for all non-overhead expenses, as well."

When he nodded that he understood, I pulled two copies of my standard contract from my case. His wife, who had obviously been lurking outside the door, came in to read it with him. While they slowly went through each clause, I looked at the life-insurance policy. It had been sold to Aaron Sommers by the Midway Agency, and it dated back, as Isaiah said, some thirty years. It was drawn on the Ajax Life Insurance company. That was a help: I had once dated the guy who now headed claims operations at Ajax. I hadn't seen him for a number of years, but I thought he would probably talk to me.

"This clause here," Margaret Sommers said, "it says you don't refund money if we don't get the results we're looking for. Is that right?"

"Yes. But you can halt the investigation at any point. Also, I will report to you after my initial inquiries, and if it doesn't seem as though they're going anywhere, I'll tell you that frankly. But that's why I ask for a five-hundred-dollar earnest payment up front: if I start to look and don't find anything, people are tempted not to pay."

"Hmmph," she said. "It doesn't seem right to me, you taking money and not delivering."

"I'm successful most of the time." I tried not to let fatigue make me cranky—she wasn't the first person to raise this point. "But it wouldn't be fair to say I always am able to find out what someone wants to know. After my first inquiry, I can estimate the amount of time it will take to complete the investigation: sometimes people see that as more than they're willing to invest. You may decide that, too."

"And you'd still keep Isaiah's five hundred dollars."

"Yes. He's hiring my professional expertise. I get paid for providing that. Just as a doctor does, even when she can't cure you." It's taken years in the business to become hard-hearted—or maybe headed—about asking for money without embarrassment.

I told them if they wanted to talk it over some more they could call me when they'd made a decision, but that I wouldn't take the uncle's policy or make any phone calls until they'd signed a contract. Isaiah Sommers said he didn't need more time, that his cousin's neighbor Camilla Rawlings had vouched for me and that was good enough for him.

Margaret Sommers folded her arms across her chest and announced that as long as Isaiah understood he was paying for it, he was free to do as he pleased; she wasn't keeping books for that mean old Jew Rubloff to throw her money away on Isaiah's useless family.

Isaiah gave her a hard look, but he signed both contracts and pulled a roll from his trousers. He counted out five hundred dollars in twenties, watching me closely while I wrote out a receipt. I signed the contracts in turn, giving one back to Isaiah, putting the other with the policy in my case. I jotted down his aunt's address and phone number, took the details for the funeral parlor, and got up to leave.

Isaiah Sommers escorted me to the door, but before he could close it I heard Margaret Sommers say, "I just hope you don't come to me when you've found yourself throwing good money after bad."

I turned down the walk on his angry response. I'd had my fill of bitterness lately, what with Lotty's arguing with Max, and now the Sommerses taking each other on. Their snarling seemed endemic to the relationship; it would be difficult to be around them often. I wondered if they had friends and what the friends did when faced with this sniping. If Max and Lotty's quarrel hardened into the same kind of misery I would find it intolerable.

Ms. Sommers's gratuitous remark about the mean old Jew she worked for also hit me hard. I don't like mean-spirited remarks of any kind, but this one jarred me, especially after listening to Max and Lotty go ten rounds on whether he should speak at today's conference. What would Margaret Sommers say if she heard Max detail his life when the Nazis came to power—forced to leave school, seeing his father compelled to kneel naked in the street? Was Lotty right, was his speaking a demeaning exposure that would do no good? Would it teach the Margaret Sommerses of the world to curb their careless prejudices?

I'd grown up a few blocks south of here, among people who would have used worse epithets than Margaret Sommers's if she'd moved next door. If she sat on a stage rehearsing the racial slurs that she probably grew up hearing, I doubted that my old neighbors would change their thinking much.

I stood on the curb, trying to stretch out the knife points in my trapezius before starting the long drive north. The curtains in the Sommerses' front window twitched. I got into my car. The September nights were drawing in; only the faintest wisp of light still stained the horizon as I turned north onto Route 41.

Why did people stay together to be unhappy? My own parents hadn't shown me a Harlequin picture of true love, but at least my mother struggled to create domestic harmony. She had married my father out of gratitude, and out of fear, an immigrant alone on the streets of the city, not knowing English. He'd been a beat cop when he rescued her in a Milwaukee Avenue bar where she'd thought she could use her grand opera training to get a job as a singer. He'd fallen in love and never, to the best of my knowledge, fallen out of it. She was affectionate toward him, but it seemed to me her true passion was reserved for me. Of course, I wasn't quite sixteen when she died: what does one know of one's parents at that age?

And what about my client's uncle? Isaiah Sommers was certain that if his uncle had cashed in his life-insurance policy, he would have told his aunt. But people have many needs for money, some of them so embarrassing that they can't bring themselves to tell their families.

My melancholy reflections had carried me unnoticing past the landmarks of my childhood, to where Route 41 became the gleaming eight-lane drive skirting the lake shore. The last color had faded from the sky, turning the lake to a spill of black ink.

At least I had a lover to turn to, even if only for a few more days: Morrell, whom I've been seeing for the past year, was leaving on Tuesday for Afghanistan. A journalist who often covers human-rights issues, he's been longing to see the Taliban up close and personal since they consolidated their power several years back.

The thought of unwinding in the comfort of his arms made me accelerate through the long dark stretch of South Lake Shore Drive, up past the bright lights of the Loop to Evanston.

III

What *Is* in a Name?

Morrell greeted me at the door with a kiss and a glass of wine. "How'd it go, Mary Poppins?"

"Mary Poppins?" I echoed blankly, then remembered Calia. "Oh, that. It was great. People think day-care workers are underpaid but that's because they don't know how much fun the job is."

I followed him into the apartment and tried not to groan out loud when I saw his editor on the couch. Not that I dislike Don Strzepek, but I'd badly wanted an evening where my conversation could be limited to an occasional snore.

"Don!" I said as he got up to shake hands. "Morrell didn't tell me to expect this pleasure. I thought you were in Spain."

"I was." He patted his shirt for cigarettes, remembered he was in a no-smoking zone, and ran his fingers through his hair instead. "I got back to New York two days ago and learned that the boy reporter was leaving for the front. So I wangled a deal with *Maverick* magazine to do a story on this Birnbaum conference and came out. Of course now I have to work for the pleasure of bidding Morrell adieu. Which I won't let you forget, amigo."

Morrell and Don had met in Guatemala when they were both covering the dirty little war there a number of years back. Don had gone on to an editorial job at Envision Press in New York, but he still undertook some reporting assignments. *Maverick* magazine, a kind of edgier version of *Harper's,* published most of his work.

"Did you get here in time for the Maccabees–EYE-team stand-off?" I asked.

"I was just telling Morrell. I picked up literature from both Posner and Durham." He waved at a pile of pamphlets on the coffee table. "I'll try to talk to both of them, but of course that's breaking news; what I need is background. Morrell says you might be able to supply me with some."

When I looked a question, he added, "I'd like a chance to meet Max Loewenthal, since he's on the national committee dealing with missing assets for Holocaust survivors. His Kindertransport story alone would make a good sidebar, and Morrell tells me that you know two of his friends who also came to England as children in the thirties."

I frowned, thinking of Lotty's furies with Max over exposing the past. "Maybe. I can introduce you to Max, but I don't know whether Dr. Herschel would want to talk to you. And Carl Tisov, Max's other friend, he's here from London on a concert tour, so whether he'd have the time, let alone the interest—"

I broke off with a shrug and picked up the pamphlets Don had brought back from the demonstrations. These included a flyer from Louis Durham, printed expensively in three colors on glossy stock. The document proclaimed opposition to the proposed Illinois Holocaust Asset Recovery Act, unless it also covered descendants of African slaves in America. Why should Illinois ban German companies who profited from the backs of Jewish and Gypsy workers but accept American companies who grew rich on the backs of African slaves?

I thought it was a good point, but I found some of the rhetoric disturbing: *It's not surprising Illinois is considering the IHARA. Jews have always known how to organize around the issue of money, and this is no exception.* Margaret Sommers's casual comment about "the mean old Jew Rubloff" echoed uncomfortably in my head.

I put the flyer back on the table and rifled through Posner's screed, which was irritating in its own way: *The day of the Jew as victim is over. We will not sit idly by while German and Swiss firms pay their shareholders with our parents' blood.*

"Ugh. Good luck in talking to these two specimens." I flipped through the rest of the literature and was surprised to see the company history Ajax Insurance had recently printed: "One Hundred Fifty Years of Life and Still Going Strong," by Amy Blount, Ph.D.

"You want to borrow it?" Don grinned.

"Thanks, I have my own copy—they held a gala a couple of weeks ago to celebrate. My most important client sits on their board, so I got chapter and verse close up. I even met the author." She'd been a thin, severe-looking young woman, dreadlocks tied back from her face with grosgrain ribbons, sipping mineral water on the fringes of a black-tie crowd. I tapped her booklet. "How'd you get this? Bull Durham going after Ajax? Or is Posner?"

Don patted his cigarette pocket again. "Both, as far as I can tell. Now that Edelweiss Re owns Ajax, Posner wants a printout of all their policies from 1933 on. And Durham is quite as insistent that Ajax open their books so he can see whom they insured from 1850 to 1865. Naturally Ajax is fighting like crazy to keep the IHARA, with or without Durham's amendment, from getting passed here or anywhere. Although the Florida and California legislation that inspired the Illinois act doesn't seem to have hurt insurers any. I guess they've figured they can stall until the last beneficiary dies. . . . Morrell, I'm going to kill in a minute if I don't get some nicotine. You cuddle Vic. I'll give my great hacking smoker's cough to warn you I'm coming back in."

"Poor guy." Morrell followed me as I went into the bedroom to change. "Mmph. I don't remember that bra."

It was a rose and silver number I rather liked myself. Morrell nuzzled my shoulder and fiddled with the hooks. After a few minutes I pulled away. "That smoker's cough is going to hack in our ears in a minute. When did you find out he was coming to town?"

"He called from the airport this morning. I tried to let you know, but your mobile phone wasn't on."

Morrell took my skirt and sweater and hung them in the closet. His extreme tidiness is a big reason I can't imagine our ever living together.

He perched on the edge of the tub when I went into the bathroom to take off my makeup. "As much as anything, I think Don wanted an excuse to get away from New York. You know, since Envision's parent company was bought by that big French firm, Gargette, he hasn't been having much fun in publishing. So many of his authors are being axed that he's afraid his job will be cut. He wants to scope out the issues surrounding the Birnbaum conference—see if there's enough in them for a book of his own."

We went back into the bedroom, where I pulled on jeans and a sweatshirt. "What about you?" I leaned against him, closing my eyes and letting the wall of fatigue I'd been battling crash over me. "Is there any risk of your contract for the Taliban book being canceled?"

"No such luck, babe." Morrell ruffled my hair. "Don't sound so hopeful."

I blushed. "I didn't mean to be so obvious. But—Kabul. An American passport is as big a liability there as a woman's exposed arms."

Morrell held me more tightly. "You're more likely to get into trouble here in Chicago than I am in Afghanistan. I've never been in love before with a woman who was beaten up and left to die on the Kennedy."

"But you could visit me every day while I was recuperating," I objected.

"I promise you, Victoria Iphigenia, that if I am left to die in the Khyber Pass, I will get Humane Medicine to fly you over so you can see me every day."

Humane Medicine was a human-rights group Morrell had traveled with in the past. They were based in Rome and were hoping to set up an inoculation program for Afghan children before the Himalayan winter set in in earnest. Morrell was going to roam around talking to anyone he could, observe the state-sanctioned boys' schools, see if he could find any of the underground girls' schools, and generally try to get some understanding of the Taliban. He'd even been taking a course on the Koran in a mosque on Devon Street.

"I'm going to fall asleep if I don't start moving," I murmured into his chest. "Let's get some dinner for Don. We've got that fettuccine I bought on the weekend. Put some tomatoes and olives and garlic in it; that'll do the job."

We went back into the living room, where Don was flipping through a copy of the *Kansas City Review*—Morrell had a critique of some recent books on Guatemala in it. "Good job, Morrell—it's a tough question, what to do about old juntas in new clothes, isn't it? Tough question to know what to do about our own government's involvement with some of these groups, too."

I drifted for a bit while they talked about South American politics. When Don announced a need for another cigarette, Morrell followed me to the kitchen to pull supper together. We ate at the island countertop in the kitchen, perched on barstools, while Don talked with a certain gloomy humor about the changes in publishing. "While I was in Barcelona, my corporate masters announced to the

Journal that writers are just content providers. Then they sent out a protocol on how to type manuscripts, demoting the content providers to clerk-typists."

A few minutes before ten he pushed his chair away from the counter. "There should be some coverage of the Birnbaum conference on the ten o'clock news. I'd like to watch, although the cameras probably concentrated on the action out front."

He helped Morrell scrape the plates into the garbage, then went to the back porch for another cigarette. While Morrell loaded the dishwasher, wiped down the counters, and wrapped leftovers in airtight containers, I went into the living room to turn on Channel 13, Global Entertainment's Chicago station. The evening anchor, Dennis Logan, was just finishing his summary of the upcoming news.

"Events turned stormy at times at the conference on Jews in America being held today at the Hotel Pleiades, but the real surprise came at the end of the afternoon from someone who wasn't even on the program. Beth Blacksin will have the whole story later in our broadcast."

I curled up in the corner of Morrell's couch. I started to nod off, but when the phone rang, I woke up to see two young women onscreen raving about a drug for yeast infections. Morrell, who'd come into the room behind me, muted the set and answered the phone.

"For you, sweet. Max." He stretched the receiver out to me.

"Victoria, I'm sorry to phone so late." Max's tone was apologetic. "We have a crisis here that I'm hoping you can solve. Ninshubur—that blue stuffed dog Calia takes everywhere—do you have it by any chance?"

I could hear Calia howling in the background, Michael shouting something, Agnes's voice raised to yell something else. I rubbed my eyes, trying to remember far enough back in the day to Calia's dog. I had stuffed Calia's day pack into my case, then forgotten about it in the harassment of getting her to Max. I put the phone down and looked around. I finally asked Morrell if he knew where my briefcase was.

"Yes, V I," he said in a voice of long-suffering. "You dropped it on the couch when you came in. I put it in my study."

I set the receiver on the couch and went down the hall to his study. My briefcase was the only thing on his desk, except for his copy of the Koran, with a long green string marking his place. Ninshubur was buried in the bottom, with some raisins, Calia's day pack, and the tale of the princess and her faithful hound. I picked up the study extension and apologized to Max, promising to run right over with the animal.

"No, no, don't disturb yourself. It's only a few blocks and I'll be glad to get out of this upheaval."

When I returned to the living room, Don said the suspense was mounting: we were on the second commercial break with the promise of fireworks to come. Max rang the bell just as Dennis Logan began speaking again.

When I let Max into the little entryway, I saw he had Carl Tisov with him. I handed the toy dog to Max, but he and Carl lingered long enough that Morrell came over to invite them in for a drink.

"Something strong, like absinthe," Carl said. "I had always wished for a large family, but after this evening's waterworks, I think I didn't miss so much. How can one small diaphragm generate more sound than an entire brass section?"

"It's the jet lag," Max said. "It always hits small ones hard."

Don called out to us to hush. "They're finally getting to the conference."

Max and Carl moved into the living room and stood behind the couch. Don turned up the volume as Beth Blacksin's pixieish face filled the screen.

"When the Southern Baptists announced their plan to send a hundred thousand missionaries to Chicago this past summer as part of their plan to convert Jews to Christianity, a lot of people were troubled, but the Birnbaum Foundation took action. Working with the Illinois Holocaust Commission, the Chicago Roman Catholic archdiocese, and Dialogue, an interfaith group here in Chicago, the foundation decided to hold a conference on issues that affect not just Illinois's substantial Jewish population but the Jewish community in America as a whole. Hence today's conference, 'Christians and Jews: a New Millennium, a New Dialogue.'

"At times, it seemed as though dialogue was the last thing on anyone's mind." The screen shifted to footage of the demonstrations out front. Blacksin gave both Posner and Durham equal sound bites, then shifted back to the hotel ballroom.

"Sessions inside the building also grew heated. The liveliest one covered the topic which sparked the demonstrations outside: the proposed Illinois Holocaust Asset Recovery Act. A panel of banking and insurance executives, arguing that the act would be so costly that all consumers would suffer, drew a lot of criticism, and a lot of anguish."

Here the screen showed furious people yelling into the mikes set up in the aisles for questions. One man shouted the insult that Margaret Sommers and Alderman Durham had both made earlier, that the reparations debate proved that all Jews ever thought about was money.

Another man yelled back that he didn't understand why Jews were considered greedy for wanting bank deposits their families had made: "Why aren't the banks called greedy? They held on to the money for sixty years and now they want to hang on to it forever." A woman stomped up to a mike to say that since the Swiss reinsurer Edelweiss had bought Ajax, she assumed Edelweiss had their own reasons to oppose the legislation.

Channel 13 let us watch the melee for about twenty seconds before Blacksin's voice cut in again. "The most startling event of the day didn't take place in the insurance session, but during one on forcible conversion, when a small man with a shy manner made the most extraordinary revelation."

We watched as a man in a suit that seemed a size too big for him spoke into one of the aisle mikes. He was closer to sixty than fifty, with greying curls that had thinned considerably at his temples.

"I want to say that it is only recently I even knew I was Jewish."

A voice from the stage asked him to identify himself.

"Oh. My name is Paul—Paul Radbuka. I was brought here after the war when I was four years old by a man who called himself my father."

Max sucked in his breath, while Carl exclaimed, "What! Who is this?"

Don and Morrell both turned to stare.

"You know him?" I asked.

Max clamped my wrist to hush me while the little figure in front of us continued to speak. "He took everything away from me, most especially my memories. Only recently have I come to know that I spent the war in Terezin, the so-called model concentration camp that the Germans named Theresienstadt. I thought I was a German, a Lutheran, like this man Ulrich who called himself my father. Only after he died, when I went through his papers, did I find out the truth. And I say it is wrong, it is criminally wrong, to take away from people the identity which is rightfully theirs."

The station let a few seconds' silence develop, then Dennis Logan, the anchor, appeared in a split screen with Beth Blacksin. "It's a most extraordinary story, Beth. You caught up with Mr. Radbuka

after the session, didn't you? We'll be showing your exclusive interview with Paul Radbuka at the end of our regular newscast. Coming
up, for fans who thought the Cubs couldn't sink lower, a surprising
come-from-ahead loss today at Wrigley."

IV

Memory Plant

Do you know him?" Don asked Max, muting the sound as yet another round of ads came up.

Max shook his head. "I know the name, but not this man. It's just—it's a most unusual name." He turned to Morrell. "If I can impose on you—I'd like to stay for the interview."

Like Max, Carl was a short man, not quite as tall as I am, but where Max smiled good-naturedly on the world around him—often amused by the human predicament—Carl held himself on alert—a bantam rooster, ready to take on all comers. Right now, he seemed edgier than usual. I looked at him but decided not to quiz him in front of Don and Morrell.

Morrell brought Max herbal tea and poured brandy for Carl. Finally the station finished its lengthy dissection of the weather and turned to Beth Blacksin. She was talking to Paul Radbuka in a small meeting room at the Pleiades. Another woman, with wings of black hair framing her oval face, was with them.

Beth Blacksin introduced herself and Paul Radbuka, then let the camera focus on the other woman. "Also here this evening is Rhea Wiell, the therapist who has treated Mr. Radbuka and helped him recover his hidden memories. Ms. Wiell has agreed to talk to me later tonight in a special edition of 'Exploring Chicago.'"

Blacksin turned to the small man. "Mr. Radbuka, how did you come to discover your true identity? You said in the meeting that it was in going through your father's papers. What did you find there?"

"The man who called himself my father," Radbuka corrected her. "It was a set of documents in code. At first I paid no attention to them. Somehow after he died I lost my own will to live. I don't understand why, because I didn't like him; he was always very brutal to me. But I became so depressed that I lost my job, I even stopped getting out of bed on many days. And then I met Rhea Wiell."

He turned to the dark-haired woman with a look of adoration. "It sounds melodramatic, but I believe I owe my life to her. And she helped me make sense of the documents, to use them to find my missing identity."

"Rhea Wiell is the therapist you found," Beth prodded him.

"Yes. She specializes in recovering memories of events that people like me block because the trauma around them is so intense."

He continued to look at Wiell, who nodded reassuringly at him. Blacksin stepped him through some of his highlights, the tormenting nightmares that he had been ashamed to speak of for fifty years, and his dawning realization that the man who called himself his father might really be someone completely unrelated to him.

"We had come to America as DP's—displaced persons—after the Second World War. I was only four, and when I was growing up, this man said we were from Germany." He gasped for air between sentences, like an asthmatic fighting to breathe. "But what I've finally learned from my work with Rhea is that his story was only half true. *He* was from Germany. But I was a—a camp child, camp survivor. I was from some other place, some country under Nazi control. This man attached himself to me in the confused aftermath of the war to get a visa to America." He looked at his hands as if he were terribly ashamed of this.

"And do you feel up to telling us about those dreams—those nightmares—that led you to Rhea Wiell?" Beth prompted him.

Wiell stroked Radbuka's hand in a reassuring fashion. He looked up again and spoke to the camera with an almost childish lack of self-consciousness.

"The nightmares were things that haunted me, things I couldn't speak out loud and could experience only in sleep. Terrible things, beatings, children falling dead in the snow, bloodstains like flowers around them. Now, thanks to Rhea, I can remember being four years old. We were moving, this strange angry man and I, we were first on a ship and then on a train. I was crying, 'My Miriam, where is my Miriam? I want my Miriam,' but the man who kept saying he was 'Vati,' my father, would hit me and finally I learned to keep all those cries to myself."

"And who was Miriam, Mr. Radbuka?" Blacksin leaned toward him, her eyes wide with empathy.

"Miriam was my little playmate, we had been together since— since I was twelve months old." Radbuka began to cry.

"When she arrived at the camp with you, isn't that right?" Beth said.

"We spent two years in Terezin together. There were six of us, the six musketeers I think of us now, but my Miriam, she was my special—I want to know she is still alive someplace, still healthy. And maybe she remembers her Paul as well." He cupped his face in his hands; his shoulders shook.

Rhea Wiell's face loomed suddenly between him and the camera. "Let's finish here, Beth. That's all Paul can handle today."

As the camera pulled back from them, Dennis Logan, the station anchor, spoke over the scene. "This sad, sad story continues to haunt not only Paul Radbuka but thousands of other Holocaust survivors. If any of you think you know Paul's Miriam, call the number on our screen, or go to our Web site, www.Globe-All.com. We'll make sure Paul Radbuka gets your message."

"How disgusting," Carl burst out when Morrell muted the set again. "How can anyone expose himself like that?"

"You sound like Lotty," Max murmured. "I suppose his hurt is so great that he isn't aware that he's exposing himself."

"People like to talk about themselves," Don put in. "That's what makes a journalist's job easy. Does his name mean something to you, Mr. Loewenthal?"

Max looked at him quizzically, wondering how Don knew his name. Morrell stepped in to perform introductions. Don explained that he had come out to cover the conference and recognized Max from today's program.

"Did you recognize the guy—Radbuka, wasn't it? The name or the person?" he added.

"You're a journalist who would like me to talk about myself to you?" Max said sharply. "I have no idea who he is."

"He was like a child," Carl said. "Utterly unself-conscious about what he was saying, even though he was recounting the most appalling events."

The phone rang again. It was Michael Loewenthal, saying that if his father had Calia's dog to please come home with it.

Max gave a guilty start. "Victoria, may I call you in the morning?"

"Of course." I went into the back to get a card from my case so that Max would have my cell-phone number, then I walked out to the car with him and Carl. "Did you two recognize the guy?"

Under the street lamp I saw Max look at Carl. "The name. I thought I recognized the name—but it doesn't seem possible. I'll call you in the morning."

When I went back inside, Don was in purdah again with a cigarette. I joined Morrell in the kitchen, where he was washing Carl's brandy glass. "Did they tell all away from the prying ears of journalism?"

I shook my head. "I'm beat, but I'm curious, too, about the therapist. Are you guys going to stay up for the special segment with her?"

"Don is panting for it. He thinks she may be his career-saving book."

"You'd better believe it," Don called through the screen door. "Although the guy would be hard to work with—his emotions seem awfully volatile."

We all returned to the living room just as the "Exploring Chicago" logo came up on the screen. The show's regular announcer said they had a special program for us tonight and turned the stage over to Beth Blacksin.

"Thank you, Dennis. In this special edition of 'Exploring Chicago,' we have the opportunity to follow up on the exciting revelations we heard earlier today, exclusively on Global Television, when a man who came here as a boy from war-torn Europe told us how therapist Rhea Wiell helped him recover memories he had buried alive for fifty years."

She ran a few segments from Radbuka's speech to the convention, followed by excerpts from her own interview with him.

"We're going to follow up on today's extraordinary story by talking to the therapist who worked with Paul Radbuka. Rhea Wiell has been having remarkable success—and started remarkable controversy, I might add—with her work in helping people get access to forgotten memories. Memories they've usually forgotten because the pain of remembering them is too great. We don't bury happy memories so deep, do we, Rhea?"

The therapist had changed into a soft green outfit that suggested an Indian mystic. She nodded with a slight smile. "We don't usually suppress memories of ice-cream sodas or romps on the beach with our friends. The memories we push away are the ones that threaten us in our core as individuals."

"Also with us is Professor Arnold Praeger, the director of the Planted Memory Foundation."

The professor was given due face time to say that we lived in an era that celebrated victims, which meant people needed to prove they had suffered more terribly than anyone else. "Such people seek out therapists who can validate their victimization. A small number of therapists have helped a large number of would-be victims remember the most shocking events: they begin recalling satanic rituals, sacrificing pets that never even existed, and so on. Many families have been terribly damaged by these planted memories."

Rhea Wiell laughed softly. "I hope you are not going to suggest that any of my patients have recovered memories of satanic sacrifices, Arnold."

"You've certainly encouraged some of them to demonize their parents, Rhea. They've ruined their parents' lives by accusing them of the most heinous brutality—accusations which can't be proved true in a court of law because the only witnesses to them are your patients' imaginations."

"You mean the only witness besides the parent who thought he was safe from ever being found out," Wiell said, keeping her voice gentle as a contrast to Praeger's sharp speech.

Praeger cut her off. "In the case of this man whose tape we just watched, the father is dead and can't even be summoned to speak on his own behalf. We're told about documents in code, but I wonder what key you used to break the code? And whether someone like me would get the same result if I looked at the documents."

Wiell shook her head, smiling gently. "My patients' privacy is sacrosanct, Arnold, you know that. These are Paul Radbuka's documents. Whether anyone else can see them is his decision alone."

Blacksin stepped in here to draw the conversation back to what recovered memories actually were. Wiell talked a little about post-traumatic stress disorder, explaining that there are a number of symptoms that people share after trauma, whether it's from battle— as soldiers or civilians—or experiencing other fragmenting events, like sexual assault.

"Children who've been sexually abused, adults who've been tortured, soldiers who've endured battle, all share some common problems: depression, inability to sleep, inability to trust people around them or form close connections."

"But people can be depressed and have sleep disorders without having been abused," Praeger snapped. "When someone comes into my office complaining of those symptoms, I am very careful about forming an opinion of the root cause: I don't immediately suggest he's been tortured by Hutu terrorists. People are at their most dependent and vulnerable with psychotherapists. It is all too easy to suggest things to them which they come ardently to believe. We like to think that our memories are objective and accurate, but unfortunately, it's very easy to create memories of events that never took place."

He went on to summarize research on planted, or created, memories that showed how people were persuaded they had taken part in marches or demonstrations when there was objective evidence that they'd never been in the city where the demonstration was held.

A little before eleven, Blacksin cut the argument short. "Until we truly understand the workings of the human mind, this debate will continue between people of goodwill. Why don't each of you take thirty seconds to summarize your positions, before we say good night. Ms. Wiell?"

Rhea Wiell looked at the camera with a wide, serious gaze. "We often like to dismiss other people's horrible memories, not because we're not compassionate. And not because we don't want to be victims. But because we're afraid to look inside ourselves. We're afraid to find out what lies hidden—what we've done to other people, or what has happened to us. It takes a lot of courage to take a journey to the past. I would never start someone on that journey who wasn't strong enough to make it to the end. I certainly never let them travel that dangerous road alone."

After that, Professor Praeger's rebuttal sounded cruel and unfeeling. If the rest of the viewing audience was like me, they wanted Wiell back, wanted her to say they were strong enough to travel to the past, and good or interesting enough that she would guide them on the way.

When the camera faded to commercials, Morrell switched off the set. Don rubbed his hands.

"This woman has book, six figures, written all over her. I'll be a hero in Paris and New York if I get her before Bertelsmann or Rupert Murdoch does. If she's legitimate. What do you two think?"

"Remember the shaman we met in Escuintla?" Morrell said to Don. "He had the same expression in his eyes. As if he saw into the most secret thoughts of your mind."

"Yes." Don shuddered. "What a horrible trip. We spent eighteen hours underneath a pigsty outwaiting the army. That was when I decided I'd be happier working full-time at Envision Press and letting people like you hog the glory, Morrell. So to speak. You think she's a charlatan?"

Morrell spread his hands. "I don't know anything about her. But she certainly believes in herself, doesn't she?"

A yawn split my face. "I'm too tired to have an opinion. But it should be easy enough to check her credentials in the morning."

I pushed myself upright on leaden legs. Morrell said he'd join me in a minute. "Before Don gets too carried away with this new book, I want to go over a few things about my own."

"In that case, Morrell, we're doing it outside. I'm not dueling with you over contracts without nicotine."

I don't know how late the two of them sat up: I was asleep almost before the door out to the porch closed behind them.

V

Sniffing for a Scent

When I got back from my run the next morning, Don was where I'd left him the night before: on the back porch with a cigarette. He was even wearing the same jeans and rumpled green shirt.

"You look horribly healthy. It makes me want to smoke more in self-defense." He sucked in a final mouthful of smoke, then ground the butt tidily on a broken piece of pottery Morrell had given him. "Morrell said you'd operate the coffee thingy for me; I suppose you know he's gone into town to see someone or other at the State Department."

I knew: Morrell had gotten up when I did, at six-thirty. As his departure date loomed, he'd stopped sleeping well—several times in the night I'd woken to find him staring rigidly at the ceiling. In the morning, I slid out of bed as quietly as possible, going to the guest bathroom in the hall to wash, then using his study to leave a message for Ralph Devereux, head of claims at Ajax Insurance, asking for a meeting at his earliest convenience. By the time I finished that, Morrell was up. While I did my stretches and drank a glass of juice, he answered his mail. When I left for my run, he was deep in an online chat with Humane Medicine in Rome.

My return route took me past Max's lakefront home. His Buick was still in the driveway, as were two other cars, presumably Carl's and Michael's rentals. There didn't seem to be any signs of life: musicians go to bed late and get up late. Max, who usually is at work by eight, must be following his son's and Carl's rhythms.

I stared at the house, as if the windows would lead me to the secret thoughts of the men inside. What had the man on television last night meant to Max and Carl? They had at least recognized the name, I was pretty sure of that. Had one of their London friends been part of the Radbuka family? But Max had made it clear last night that he wasn't ready to talk about that. I shouldn't try to trespass. I shook out my legs and finished my run.

Morrell had a semicommercial espresso machine. Back in his apartment, I made cappuccinos for Don and myself before showering. While I dressed, I checked my own messages. Ralph had called from Ajax and would be delighted to squeeze me in at a quarter of twelve. I put on the rose silk sweater and sage skirt I'd worn yesterday. It gets complicated spending part of my life at Morrell's—the clothes I want are always in my own apartment when I'm with him, or in his place when I'm home.

Don had moved to the kitchen eating island with the *Herald-Star* when I came in. "If they took you for a ride on a Russian mountain in Paris, where would you be?"

"Russian mountain?" I mixed yogurt and granola with orange slices. "Is this helping you get ready to ask searching comments of Posner and Durham?"

He grinned. "I'm sharpening my wits. If you were going to do some fast checking on the therapist who was on television last night, where would you start?"

I leaned against the counter while I ate. "I'd search the accreditation databases for therapists to see if she was licensed and what her training was. I'd go to ProQuest—she and the guy from the memory foundation have been mixing it up—there might be some articles about her."

Don scribbled a note on the corner of the crossword-puzzle clues. "How long would it take you to do it for me? And how much would you charge?"

"Depends on how deep you wanted to go. The basics I could do pretty fast, but I charge a hundred dollars an hour with a five-hour initial minimum. How generous is Gargette's expenses policy?"

He tossed the pencil aside. "They have four hundred cost accountants in their head office at Rheims just to make sure editors like me don't eat more than a Big Mac on the road, so they're not too likely to spring for a private investigator. Still, this could be a really big book. If she is who she says she is—if the guy is who he says he is. Could you do some checking for me on spec?"

I was about to agree when I thought of Isaiah Sommers, carefully counting out his twenties. I shook my head unhappily. "I can't make exceptions for friends. It makes it hard for me to charge strangers."

He pulled out a cigarette and tapped it on the paper. "Okay. Can you do some checking and trust me for the money?"

I grimaced. "Yeah. I guess. I'll bring a contract back with me tonight."

He returned to the porch. I finished my breakfast and ran water over the bowl—Morrell would have a fit if he came home to find case-hardened yogurt on it—then followed Don out the back door: my car was parked in the alley behind the building. Don was reading the news but looked up to say good-bye. On my way down the back stairs the word came to me from nowhere. "Roller coaster. If it's the same in French as Italian, a Russian mountain is a roller coaster."

"You've already earned your fee." He picked up his pencil and turned back to the crossword page.

Before going to my office, I swung by Global Entertainment's studios on Huron Street. When the company moved into town a year ago, they bought a skyscraper in the hot corridor just northwest of the river. Their Midwest regional offices, where they control everything from a hundred seventy newspapers to a big chunk of the broadband DSL business, are on the upper levels, with their studios on the ground floor.

Global executives are not my biggest fans in Chicago, but I've worked with Beth Blacksin since before the company took over Channel 13. She was on the premises, editing a segment for the evening news. She ran out to the lobby in the sloppy jeans she can't wear on-air, greeting me like a long-lost friend—or, anyway, a valuable source.

"I was riveted by your interview yesterday with that guy Radbuka," I said. "How'd you find him?"

"Warshawski!" Her expressive face came alive with excitement. "Don't tell me he's been murdered. I'm getting to a live mike."

"Calm down, my little newshound. As far as I know he's still on the planet. What can you tell me about him?"

"You've found out who the mysterious Miriam is, then."

I took her by the shoulders. "Blacksin, calm down—if you're able. I'm purely on a fishing expedition right now. Do you have an address you'd be willing to give out? For him, or for the therapist?"

She took me with her past the security station to a warren of cubicles where the news staff had desks. She went through a stack of papers next to her computer and found the standard waiver sheet people sign when they give interviews. Radbuka had listed a suite number at an address on North Michigan, which I copied down. His signature was large and untidy, kind of the way he'd looked in his too-big suit. Rhea Wiell, by contrast, wrote in a square, almost print-like hand. I copied out the spelling of her name. And then noticed that Radbuka's address was the same as hers. Her office at Water Tower.

"Could you get me a copy of the tape? Your interview, and the discussion between the therapist and the guy from the antihypnosis place? That was good work, pulling them together at the last minute."

She grinned. "My agent's happy—my contract's coming up in six weeks. Praeger has a real bee in his bonnet about Wiell. They've been adversaries on a bunch of cases, not just in Chicago but all around the country. He thinks she's the devil incarnate and she thinks he's the next thing to a child molester himself. They've both had media training—they looked civilized on camera, but you should have heard them when the camera wasn't rolling."

"What did you think of Radbuka?" I asked. "Up close and personal, did you believe his story?"

"Do you have proof he's a fraud? Is that what this is really about?"

I groaned. "I don't know anything about him. Zippo. Niente. Nada. I can't say it in any more languages. What was your take on him?"

Her eyes opened wide. "Oh, Vic, I believed him completely. It was one of the most harrowing interviews I've ever done—and I talked to people after Lockerbie. Can you imagine growing up the way he did and then finding the man who claimed to be your father was like your worst enemy?"

"What was his father—foster father's name?"

She scrolled through the text on her screen. "Ulrich. Whenever Paul referred to him, he always used the man's German name, instead of 'Daddy' or 'Father' or something."

"Do you know what he found in Ulrich's papers that made him realize his lost identity? In the interview he said they were in code."

She shook her head, still looking at the screen. "He talked about working it through with Rhea and getting the correct interpretation. He said they proved to him that Ulrich had really been a Nazi collaborator. He talked a lot about how brutal Ulrich had been to him, beating him for acting like a sissy, locking him in a closet when he was away at work, sending him to bed without food."

"There wasn't a woman on the scene? Or was she a participant in the abuse?" I asked.

"Paul says Ulrich told him that his mother—or Mrs. Ulrich, anyway—had died in the bombing of Vienna as the war was ending. I don't think Mr. Ulrich ever married here, or even had women to the house. Ulrich and Paul seemed to have been a real pair of loners. Papa went to work, came home, beat Paul. Paul was supposed to be a doctor, but he couldn't handle pressure, so he ended up as an X-ray technician, which earned more ridicule. He never moved out of his father's house. Isn't that creepy? Staying with him even when he was big enough to earn his own living?"

That was all she could, or at least all she would, tell me. She promised to messenger over a tape of the various segments with Radbuka, as well as the meeting between the therapists, to my office later in the day.

I still had time before my appointment at Ajax to do some work in my office. It was only a few miles north and west of Global—but a light-year away in ambience. No glass towers for me. Three years ago a sculptor friend had invited me to share a seven-year lease with her for a converted warehouse on Leavitt. Since the building was a fifteen-minute drive from the financial district where most of my business lies and the rent was half what you pay in those gleaming high-rises, I'd signed on eagerly.

When we moved in, the area was still a grimy no-man's-land between the Latino neighborhood farther west and a slick Yuppie area nearer the lake. At that time, bodegas and palm readers vied with music stores for the few retail spaces in what had been an industrial zone. Parking abounded. Even though the Yuppies are starting to move in, building espresso bars and boutiques, we still have plenty of collapsing buildings and drunks. I was against further gentrification—I didn't want to see my rent skyrocket when the current lease expired.

Tessa's truck was already in our little lot when I pulled in. She'd received a major commission last month and was putting in long hours to build a model of both the piece and the plaza it would occupy. When I passed her studio door she was perched at her outsize drafting table, sketching. She's testy if interrupted, so I went down the hall to my own office without speaking.

I made a couple of copies of Isaiah Sommers's uncle's policy and locked the original in my office safe, where I keep all client documents during an active investigation. It's really a strongroom, with fireproof walls and a good sturdy door.

Midway Insurance's address was listed on the policy: they had sold the policy to Aaron Sommers all those years back. If I couldn't get satisfaction from the company, I'd have to go back to the agent—and hope he remembered what he'd done thirty years ago. I checked the phone book. The agency was still on Fifty-third Street, down in Hyde Park.

I had two queries to complete for bread-and-butter clients. While I sat on hold with the Board of Health, I logged on to Lexis and Pro-Quest and submitted a search on Rhea Wiell, as well as Paul Radbuka.

My Board of Health connection came on the phone and for once answered all my questions without a lot of hedging. When I'd wrapped up my report I checked back with Lexis. There was nothing on the Radbuka name. I checked my disks of phone numbers and addresses for the U.S.—more up-to-date than Web search engines—and found nothing. When I looked up his father's name, Ulrich, I got forty-seven matches in the Chicago area. Maybe Paul hadn't changed his name legally when he became Radbuka.

Rhea Wiell, on the other hand, gave me a lot of hits. She had apparently appeared as an expert witness in a number of trials, but tracking them down so I could get transcripts would be a tedious business. However, I did find she was a clinical social worker, fully accredited by the State of Illinois: at least she had started from an authentic position. I logged off and swept my papers together into my case so I could be on time for my meeting with the head of the Ajax claims department.

VI

Staking a Claim

I originally met Ralph Devereux early in my life as an investigator. It hasn't been so many years, but at the time I was the first woman in Chicago, maybe even the country, with a PI license. It was a struggle to get clients or witnesses to treat me seriously. When Ralph took a bullet in his shoulder because he couldn't believe his boss was a crook, our relationship fractured as abruptly as his scapula.

I hadn't seen him since; I admit I felt a little nervous anticipation as I rode the L down to Ajax's headquarters on Adams Street. When I got off the elevator at the sixty-third floor, I even stopped in the ladies' room to make sure my hair was combed and my lipstick tidily confined to my mouth.

The executive-floor attendant escorted me down a mile of parquet to Ralph's corner; his secretary pronounced my name perfectly and buzzed the inner sanctum. Ralph emerged smiling, both arms held out in greeting.

I took his hands in my own, smiling back, trying to hide a twinge of sadness. When I'd met him, Ralph had been a slim-hipped, ardent young man with a shock of black hair falling in his eyes and an engaging grin. His hair was still thick, although liberally tinged with grey, but he had jowls now, and while he wasn't exactly fat, those slim hips had disappeared into the same past as our brief affair.

I exchanged conventional greetings, congratulating him on his promotion to head of the claims department. "It looks as though you recovered full use of your arm," I added.

"Just about. It still bothers me when the weather's damp. I got so depressed after that injury—waiting for it to heal, feeling like a moron for letting it happen at all—that I took to cheeseburgers. The big shake-ups here the last few years haven't helped any, either. You look great, though. You still running five miles every morning? Maybe I should hire you to coach me."

I laughed. "You're already in your first meeting before I get out of bed. You'd have to take a lower-pressure job. The shake-ups you mentioned—those from Edelweiss acquiring Ajax?"

"That came at the end, really. We took a lot of hits in the market at the same time that Hurricane Andrew overwhelmed us. While we were dealing with that, and laying off a fifth of our workforce worldwide, Edelweiss snapped up a chunk of our depressed stock. They were a hostile suitor—I'm sure you followed that in the financial pages—but they certainly haven't been a hostile master. They seem quite eager to learn how we do things here, rather than wanting to interfere. In fact, the managing director from Zurich who's looking after Ajax wanted to sit in on my meeting with you."

His hand in the small of my back, he ushered me into his office, where a man with tortoiseshell glasses, dressed in a pale wool suit and a bold tie, stood when I entered. He was around forty, with a round merry face that seemed to match the tie more than the suit.

"Vic Warshawski, Bertrand Rossy from Edelweiss Re in Zurich. You two should get along well—Vic speaks Italian."

"Oh, really?" Rossy shook hands. "With the name Warshawski I would have assumed Polish."

"My mother was from Pitigliano—*vicino* Orvieto," I said. "I can only stumble through a few stock phrases of Polish."

Rossy and I sat in chrome tube chairs next to a glass-topped table. Ralph himself, who had always had an incongruous-seeming taste for modernism, leaned against the edge of the aluminum tabletop he used as a desk.

I asked Rossy the usual things, about where he had acquired his perfect English (he had gone to school in England) and how he liked Chicago (very much). His wife, who was Italian, had found the summer weather oppressive and had taken their two children to her family's estate in the hills above Bologna.

"She just returned this week with Paolo and Marguerita for the start of the school year here and already I'm better dressed than I was all summer, isn't that right, Devereux? I could barely persuade her to let me out the front door in this tie this morning." He laughed loudly, showing dimples at the corners of his mouth. "Now I make a campaign to persuade her to try the Chicago opera: her family have been in the same box at La Scala since it opened in 1778 and she can't believe a raw young city like this can really produce opera."

I told him I went to a production once a year in tribute to my mother, who had taken me every fall, but of course I couldn't compare it to a European opera company. "Nor do I have a family box: it's the upper gallery for me, what we call the nosebleed section."

He laughed again. "Nosebleed section. My colloquial American is going to improve for talking to you. We shall all go together one evening, if you can condescend to climb down from the nosebleed section. But I see Devereux looking at his watch—oh, very discreetly, don't be embarrassed, Devereux. A beautiful woman is an inducement to waste precious business minutes, but Miss Warshawski must have come here for some other purpose than to discuss opera."

I pulled out the photocopy of the Aaron Sommers policy and explained the events around his aborted funeral. "I thought if I came straight to you with the situation, you could get me an answer fast."

When Ralph took the photocopy out to his secretary, I asked Rossy if he'd attended yesterday's Birnbaum conference. "Friends of mine were involved. I'm wondering if Edelweiss is concerned about the proposed Holocaust Asset Recovery Act."

Rossy put his fingertips together. "Our position is in line with the industry, that however legitimate the grief and the grievances—of both the Jewish and the African-American communities—the expense of a policy search shall be most costly for all policyholders. For our own company, we don't worry about the exposure. Edelweiss was only a small regional insurer during the war, so the likelihood of involvement with large numbers of Jewish claimants is small.

"Of course, now I'm learning that we do have this fifteen-year history of slavery still taking place in America while Ajax was in its early days. And I am just now suggesting to Ralph that we get Ms. Blount, the woman who wrote our little history, to look in the archives so we know who our customers were in those very old days. Assuming she has not already decided to send our archives to this Alderman Durham. But how expensive it is to go back to the past. How very costly, indeed."

"Your history? Oh, that booklet on 'One Hundred Fifty Years of Life.' I have a copy—which I confess I've yet to read. Does it cover

Ajax's pre-Emancipation years? Do you really think Ms. Blount would hand your documents to an outsider?"

"Is this the true reason for your visit here? Ralph says you are a detective. Are you doing something very subtle, very Humphrey Bogart, pretending to care about the Sommers claim and trying to trick me with questions about the Holocaust and slavery claims? I did think this little policy was small, small potatoes for you to bring to the director of claims." He smiled widely, inviting me to treat this as a joke if I wanted to.

"I'm sure in Switzerland as well as here people call on those they know," I said. "Ralph and I worked together a number of years ago, before he became so exalted, so I'm taking advantage of our relationship in the hopes of a fast answer for my client."

"*Exalted's* the word for me," Ralph came back in. "And Vic has such a depressing habit of being right about financial crime that it's easier to go along with her from the start than fight her."

"What crime surrounds this claim, then—what are you correct about today?" Rossy asked.

"So far, nothing, but I haven't had time to consult a psychic yet."

"Psychic?" he repeated doubtfully.

"*Indovina,*" I grinned. "They abound in the area where I have my office."

"Ah, psychic," Rossy exclaimed. "I have been pronouncing it wrong all these years. I must remember to tell my wife about this. She is keenly interested in unusual events in my business day. Psychics and nosebleeds. She will enjoy them so much."

I was saved from trying to respond by Ralph's secretary, who ushered in a young woman clutching a thick file. She was wearing khaki jeans and a sweater that had shrunk from too many washings.

"This is Connie Ingram, Mr. Devereux," the secretary said. "She has the information you wanted."

Ralph didn't introduce Rossy or me to Ms. Ingram. She blinked at us unhappily but showed her packet to Ralph.

"This here is all the documents on L-146938-72. I'm sorry about being in my jeans and all, but my supervisor is away, so they told me to bring the file up myself. I printed the financials from off the microfiche, so they aren't as clear as they could be, but I did the best I could."

Bertrand Rossy joined me when I got up to look over her shoulder at the papers. Connie Ingram flipped through the pages until she came to the payment documents.

Ralph pulled them out of the file and studied them. He looked at them for a long moment, then turned to me sternly. "It seems that your client's family was trying to collect twice on the same policy, Vic. We frown on that here."

I took the pages from him. The policy had been paid up in 1986. In 1991, someone had submitted a death certificate. A photocopy of the canceled check was attached. It had been paid to Gertrude Sommers, care of the Midway Insurance Agency, and duly endorsed by them.

For a moment, I was too dumbfounded to speak. The grieving widow must be quite a con artist to convince the nephew into shelling out for his uncle's funeral when she'd collected on the policy a decade ago. But how on earth had she gotten a death certificate back then? My first coherent thought was mean-spirited: I was glad I'd insisted on earnest money up front. I doubted Isaiah Sommers would have paid to learn this bit of news.

"This isn't your idea of a joke, is it, Vic?" Ralph demanded.

He was angry because he thought he looked foolishly incompetent in front of his new master: I wasn't going to ride him. "Scout's honor, Ralph. The story I told you is the identical one I got from my client. Have you ever seen something like this before? A fraudulent death certificate?"

"It happens." He flicked a glance at Rossy. "Usually it's someone faking his own death to get away from creditors. And then the circumstances of the policy—the size—the timing between when it was sold and when it was cashed—make us investigate before we pay. For something like this"—he snapped the canceled check with his middle finger—"we wouldn't investigate such a small face value—and one where we'd collected all the premium years before."

"So the possibility exists? The possibility that people are submitting claims that aren't rightfully theirs?" Rossy took the whole file from Ralph and started going through it one page at a time.

"But the company would only pay once," Ralph said. "As you can see, we had all the information available when the funeral home submitted the policy, so we didn't pay the claim twice. I don't suppose anyone from the agency would have bothered to check whether the purchaser"—he looked at the tab on the file—"whether Sommers was really dead when his wife filed the claim."

Connie Ingram asked doubtfully if she should talk to her supervisor about calling the agency or the funeral home. Ralph turned to me. "Are you going to talk to them anyway, Vic? Will you let Connie know what you find out? The truth, I mean, not some version that you want Ajax to learn?"

"If Miss Warshawski is in the habit of hiding her findings from the company, Ralph, perhaps we shouldn't trust her with these delicate questions." Rossy gave me a little bow. "I'm sure you would ask your questions so skillfully that our agent might be startled into telling you—what he ought to keep between himself and the company."

Ralph started to say that he was only trying to bait me, then sighed and told Connie by all means to ask any questions she needed to reclose the file.

"Ralph, what if someone else filed the claim, someone pretending to be Gertrude Sommers," I said. "Would the company make her whole?"

Ralph rubbed the deepening crease between his eyes. "Don't ask me to make moral decisions without the facts. What if it was her husband—or her kid? He's listed as a secondary beneficiary after her. Or her minister? I'm not going to commit the company to anything until I know the truth."

He was talking to me but looking at Rossy, who was looking at his watch, not at all discreetly. Ralph muttered something about their next appointment. This made me more uneasy even than the fraud over the claim: I don't like my lovers, even long-former lovers, to feel the need to be obsequious.

As I left the office, I asked Ralph for a photocopy of the canceled check and the death certificate. Rossy answered for him. "These are company documents, Devereux."

"But if you don't let me show them to my client, then he has no way of knowing whether I'm lying to him," I said. "You remember the case this last spring, where various life-insurance companies admitted to charging black customers as much as four times the amount they did whites? I assure you, that will leap into my client's mind. And then, instead of me coming around asking for documents in a nice way, you might have a federal lawsuit with a subpoena attached."

Rossy stared at me, suddenly frosty. "If the threat of a lawsuit seems to your mind to be 'asking in a nice way,' then I have to ask myself questions about your business practices."

With the dimples in abeyance, he showed he could be a formidable corporate presence. I smiled and took his hand, turning it to look at the palm. He was startled into standing motionless.

"Signor Rossy, I wasn't threatening you with a lawsuit: I was an *indovina,* reading your fortune, foreseeing an inevitable future."

The frost melted abruptly. "What other things do you divine?"

I put his hand down. "My powers are limited. But you seem to have a long lifeline. Now, with your permission may I copy the canceled check and the death certificate?"

"Forgive my Swiss habits of being unwilling to part with official documents. By all means, make copies of these two papers. But the file as a whole I think I'll keep with me. Just in case your charm makes you more persuasive with this young lady than her normal loyalties would allow you to be."

He gestured at Connie Ingram, who blushed. "Sir, I'm really sorry, sir, but can you fill out a slip for me? I can't let a claim file stay out of our area without a notice of the number and of who has it."

"Ah, so you have respect for documents as well. Excellent. You write down what you need, and I will sign it. Will that fulfill the requirements?"

Her color spreading to her collarbone, Connie Ingram went out to Ralph's secretary to type up what she needed. I followed with the documents I was allowed to have; Ralph's secretary copied them for me.

Ralph walked partway down the hall with me. "Stay in touch, Vic, okay? I would be grateful to hear from you if you learn anything about this business."

"You'll be the second to know," I promised. "You going to be equally forthcoming?"

"Naturally." He grinned, briefly showing a trace of the old Ralph. "And if I remember right, I'm likely to be much more forthcoming than you."

I laughed, but I still felt sad as I waited for the elevator. When the doors finally opened with a subdued *ding,* a young woman in a prim tweed suit stepped off, clutching a tan briefcase to her side. The dreadlocks tidily pulled away from her face made me blink in recognition.

"Ms. Blount—I'm V I Warshawski—we met at the Ajax gala a month ago."

She nodded and briefly touched my fingertips. "I need to be in a meeting."

"Ah, yes: with Bertrand Rossy." I thought of putting her on her guard against Rossy's accusation that she was siphoning off company documents for Bull Durham, but she whisked herself down the hall toward Ralph's office before I could make up my mind.

The elevator that brought her had left. Before another arrived, Connie Ingram joined me, her paperwork apparently finished.

"Mr. Rossy seems very protective of his documents," I commented.

"We can't afford to misplace any paper around here," she said primly. "People can sue us if we don't have our records in tiptop shape."

"Are you worried about a suit from the Sommers family?"

"Mr. Devereux said the agent was responsible for the claim. So it's not our problem here at the company, but of course he and Mr. Rossy—"

She stopped, red-faced, as if remembering Rossy's comment about my persuasive charms. The elevator arrived and she scurried into it. It was twelve-forty, heart of the lunch hour. The elevator stopped every two or three floors to take in people before making its express descent from forty to the ground. I wondered what indiscretion she had bitten back, but there wasn't any way I could pump her.

Something there is that doesn't love a fence," I muttered as I boarded the northbound L. Lots of people on the train were muttering to themselves: I fit right in. "When someone is guarding documents, is it because his corporate culture is obsessive, as Rossy said? Or because there's something in them he doesn't want me to see?"

"Because he's in the pay of the U-nited Nations," the man next to me said. "They're bringing in tanks. Those U-nited Nations helie-copters landing in Dee-troit, I seen them on TV."

"You're right," I said to his beery face. "It's definitely a UN plot. So you think I should go down to Midway Insurance, talk to the agent, see if my charms are persuasive enough to wangle a look at the sales file?"

"Your charms plenty persuasive enough for me," he leered.

That was esteem-enhancing. When I got off the train at Western, I picked up my car and immediately headed south again. Down in Hyde Park, I found a meter with forty minutes on it on one of the side streets near the bank where Midway Insurance had their offices. The bank building itself was the neighborhood's venerable dowager, its ten stories towering over Hyde Park's main shopping street. The facade had recently been cleaned up, but once I got off the elevator onto the sixth floor, the dim lights and dingy walls betrayed a management indifference to tenant comfort.

Midway Insurance was wedged between a dentist and a gynecologist. The black letters on the door, telling me they insured life, home, and auto, had been there a long time: part of the *H* in *Home* had peeled away, so that it looked as though Midway insured *nome*.

The door was locked, but when I rang the bell someone buzzed me in. The office beyond was even drearier than the hall. The flickering fluorescent light was so dim that I didn't notice a peeling corner of linoleum until I'd tripped on it. I grabbed at a filing cabinet to keep from falling.

"Sorry—I keep meaning to fix that." I hadn't noticed the man until he spoke—he was sitting at a desk that took up most of the room, but the light was bad enough I hadn't seen him when I opened the door.

"I hope you buy premises insurance, because you're inviting a nasty suit if you don't glue that down," I snapped, coming all the way into the room.

He turned on a desk lamp, revealing a face with freckles so thick that they formed an orange carpet across his face. At my words the carpet turned a deeper red.

"I don't get much walk-in business," he explained. "Most of the time we're in the field."

I looked around, but there wasn't a desk for a second person. I moved a phone book from the only other chair and sat down. "You have partners? Subordinates?"

"I inherited the business from my dad. He died three years ago, but I keep forgetting that. I think the business is going to die, too. I never have been much good with cold calls, and now the Internet is killing independent agents."

Mentioning the Internet reminded him that his computer was on. He flicked a key to start the screensaver, but before the fish began cascading I saw he'd been playing some kind of solitaire.

The computer was the only newish item in the room. His desk was a heavy yellow wooden one, the kind popular fifty years ago, with two rows of drawers framing a kneehole for the user's legs. Black stains from decades of grime, coffee, ink, and who knows what scarred the yellow in the places I could see it—most of the surface was covered in a depressing mass of paper. My own office looked monastic by comparison.

Four large filing cabinets took up most of the remaining space. A curling poster of the Chinese national table-tennis team provided the only decoration. A large pot hung from a chain above the window, but the plant within had withered down to a few drying leaves.

He sat up and tried to put a semblance of energy into his tone. "What can I do for you?"

"I'm V I Warshawski." I handed him one of my cards. "And you are?"

"Fepple. Howard Fepple." He looked at my card. "Oh. The detective. They told me you'd be calling."

I looked at my watch. It had been just over an hour since I left Ajax. Someone in the company had moved fast.

"Who told you that? Bertrand Rossy?"

"I don't know the name. It was one of the girls in claims."

"Women," I corrected irritably.

"Whatever. Anyway, she told me you'd be asking about one of our old policies. Which I can't tell you anything about, because I was in high school when it was sold."

"So you looked it up? What did it tell you about who cashed it in?"

He leaned back in his chair, the man at ease. "I can't see why that's any of your business."

I grinned evilly, all ideas about charm and persuasion totally forgotten. "The Sommers family, whom I represent, have an interest in this matter that could be satisfied by a federal lawsuit. Involving subpoenas for the files and suing the agency for fraud. Maybe your father sold the policy to Aaron Sommers back in 1971, but you own the agency now. It wouldn't be the Internet that would finish you off."

His fleshy lips pursed together in a pout. "For your information it wasn't my father who sold the policy but Rick Hoffman, who worked for him here."

"So where can I find Mr. Hoffman?"

He smirked. "Wherever you look for the dead. But I don't imagine old Rick ended up in heaven. He was a mean SOB. How he did as well as he did . . ." He shrugged eloquently.

"You mean unlike you he wasn't afraid of the cold call?"

"He was a Friday man. You know, going into the poor neighborhoods on Friday afternoons collecting after people got paid. A lot of our business is life insurance like that, small face value, enough to get someone buried right and leave a little for the family. It's all someone like this Sommers could probably afford, ten thousand, although that was big by our standards, usually they're only three or four thousand."

"So Hoffman collected from Aaron Sommers. Had he paid up the policy?"

Fepple tapped a file on top of the mess of papers. "Oh, yes. Yes, it took him fifteen years, but it was paid in full. The beneficiaries were his wife, Gertrude, and his son, Marcus."

"So who cashed it in? And if they did, how come the family still had the policy?"

Looking at me resentfully, Fepple started through the file, page by page. He stopped at one point, staring at a document, his lips moving soundlessly. A little smile flickered at the corners of his mouth, an unpleasant, secretive smile, but after a moment he continued the search. Finally he pulled out the same documents I'd already seen at the company: a copy of the death certificate and a copy of the countersigned check.

"What else was in the file?" I asked.

"Nothing," he said quickly. "There was nothing unusual about it at all. Rick did a zillion of these little weekend sales. There's no surprise to them."

I didn't believe him, but I didn't have a way to call his bluff. "Not much of a way to make a living, three- and four-thousand-dollar sales."

"Rick did real well for himself. He knew how to work the angles, I'll tell you that much."

"And what you're not telling me?"

"I'm not telling you my private business. You've barged in here without an appointment, fishing around for dirt, but you don't have any grounds to ask questions. And don't go waving federal lawsuits at me. If there was any funny business about this, it was the company's responsibility, not mine."

"Did Hoffman have any family?"

"A son. I don't know what happened to him—he was a whole lot older than me, and he and old Rick didn't hit it off too great. I had to go to the funeral, with my old man, and we were the only damned people in the church. The son was long gone by then."

"So who inherited Hoffman's share of the business?"

Fepple shook his head. "He wasn't a partner. He worked for my old man. Strictly commission, but—he did well."

"So why don't you pick up his client list and carry on for him?"

The nasty little smile reappeared. "I might just do that very thing. I didn't realize until the company called me what a little gold mine Rick's way of doing business represented."

I wanted to see that file badly, but short of grabbing it from the desk and running off down the stairs into the arms of the guard in the lobby, I couldn't think of any way to look at it. At least, not at the moment. As I left, I tripped again on the corner of the linoleum. If Fepple didn't fix it soon I'd be suing him myself.

Since I was already south, I went on another two miles to Sixty-seventh Street, where the Delaney Funeral Parlor stood. It was in an imposing white building, easily the grandest on the block, with four hearses parked in the lot behind it. I left my Mustang next to them and went in to see what I could learn.

Old Mr. Delaney talked to me himself, about how sorry they were to have had to inflict such grief on a sweet decent woman like Sister Sommers but that he couldn't afford to bury people for charity: if you did it once, every freeloader on the South Side would be coming around with some story or other about their insurance falling through. As to how he'd learned that Sommers's policy had already been cashed in, they had a simple procedure with the life-insurance companies. They had called, given the policy number, and been told that the policy had already been paid. I asked who he'd spoken to.

"I don't give anything away free, young lady," Mr. Delaney said austerely. "If you want to pursue your own inquiries at the company, I urge you to do so, but don't expect me to give you for nothing information I spent my hard-earned money finding out. All I will tell you is that it isn't the first time this has happened, that a bereaved family has discovered that their loved one had disposed of his resources without privileging them with the information. It isn't a regular occurrence, but families are often sadly surprised at the behavior of their loved ones. Human nature can be all too human."

"A lesson I'm sure Gertrude Sommers and her nephew learned at Aaron Sommers's funeral," I said, getting up to leave.

He bowed his head mournfully, as if unaware of the bite behind my words. He hadn't gotten to be one of the richest men in South Shore by apologizing for his rigorous business methods.

VIII

Tales of Hoffman

The score so far today seemed to be Warshawski zero, visitors three. I hadn't gotten any satisfaction from Ajax, or the Midway Agency, or the funeral director. While I was south, I might as well complete my sweep of frustrating meetings by visiting the widow.

She lived a few blocks from the Dan Ryan Expressway, in a rickety twelve-flat with a burnt-out building on one side and a lot with bits of masonry and rusted-out cars on the other. A couple of guys were leaning over the engine of an elderly Chevy when I pulled up. The only other person on the street was a fierce-looking woman muttering as she sucked from a brown paper bag.

The Sommerses' doorbell didn't seem to work, but the street door hung loosely on its hinges, so I went on into the building. The stairwell smelled of urine and stale grease. Dogs barked from behind several doors as I passed, briefly overwhelming the thin hopeless wail of a baby. I was so depressed by the time I reached Gertrude Sommers's door that I was hard put to knock instead of beating a craven retreat.

A few minutes passed. Finally I heard a slow step and a deep voice calling to know who it was. I told her my name, that I was the detective her nephew had hired. She scraped back the three dead bolts holding the door and stood in the entrance for a moment, looking me over somberly before letting me in.

Gertrude Sommers was a tall woman. Even in old age she was a good two inches taller than my five-eight, and even in grief she held herself erect. She was wearing a dark dress that rustled when she walked. A black lace handkerchief, tucked in the cuff of her left sleeve, underscored her mourning. Looking at her made me feel grubby in my work-worn skirt and sweater.

I followed her into the apartment's main room, standing until she pointed regally at the sofa. The bright floral upholstery was shielded in heavy plastic, which crackled loudly when I sat down.

The building's squalor ended on her doorstep. Every surface that wasn't encased in plastic shone with polish, from the dining table against the far wall to the clock with its fake chimes over the television. The walls were hung with pictures, many of the same smiling child, and a formal shot of my client and his wife on their wedding day. To my surprise, Alderman Durham was on the wall—once in a solo shot, and again with his arms around two young teens in his blue Empower Youth Energy sweatshirts. One of the boys was leaning on metal crutches, but both were beaming proudly.

"I'm sorry for your loss, Ms. Sommers. And sorry for the terrible mix-up over your husband's life insurance."

She folded her lips tightly. She wasn't going to help.

I plowed ahead as best I could, laying the photocopies of the fraudulent death certificate and canceled insurance check in front of her. "I'm bewildered by this situation. I'm wondering if you have any suggestions about how it could have occurred."

She refused to look at the documents. "How much did they pay you to come here and accuse me?"

"No one paid me to do that, and no one could pay me to do that, Ms. Sommers."

"Easy words, easy words for you to say, young woman."

"True enough." I paused, trying to feel my way into her point of view. "My mother died when I was fifteen. If some stranger had cashed in her burial policy and then accused my dad of doing it, well, I can imagine what he would have done, and he was an easygoing guy. But if I can't ask you any questions about this, how am I ever going to find out who cashed this policy all those years ago?"

She clamped her lips together, thinking it over, then said, "Have you talked to the insurance man, that Mr. Hoffman who came around every Friday afternoon before Mr. Sommers could spend his pay on drink, or whatever he imagined a poor black man would do instead of putting food on his family's table?"

"Mr. Hoffman is dead. The agency is in the hands of the previous owner's son, who doesn't seem to know too much about the business. Did Mr. Hoffman treat your husband with disrespect?"

She sniffed. "We weren't people to him. We were ticks in that book he carried around with him. Driving up in that big Mercedes like he did, we knew just where our hard-saved nickels went. And no way to question whether he was honest or not."

"You think now he cheated you?"

"How else do you explain this?" She slapped the papers on the table, still without looking at them. "You think I am deaf, dumb, and blind? I know what goes on in this country with black folk and insurance. I read how that company in the south got caught charging black folk more than their policies were worth."

"Did that happen to you?"

"No. But we paid. We paid and we paid and we paid. All to have it go up in smoke."

"If you didn't file the claim in 1991, and you don't think your husband did, who would have?" I asked.

She shook her head, but her gaze inadvertently went to the wall of photographs.

I drew a breath. "This isn't easy to ask, but your son was listed on the policy."

Her look scorched me. "My son, my son died. It was because of him we went after a bigger policy, thinking to leave him a little something besides our funerals, Mr. Sommers's and mine. Muscular dystrophy, our boy had. And in case you're thinking, Oh, well, they cashed the policy to pay his medical bills, let me tell you, miss, Mr. Sommers worked two shifts for four years, paying those bills. I had to quit my job to take care of my son when he got too sick to move anymore. After he passed, I worked two shifts, too, to get rid of the bills. At the nursing home where I was an aide. If you're going to pry into all my private details you can have that one without charging my nephew a nickel for it: the Grand Crossing Elder Care Home. But you can go snooping through my life. Maybe I have a secret *drinking* vice—you'll go ask them at the church where I became a Christian and where my husband was a deacon for forty-five years. Maybe Mr. Sommers *gambled* and used all my housekeeping money. That's the way you plan on ruining my reputation, isn't it."

I looked at her steadily. "So you won't let me ask you any questions about the policy. And you can't think of anyone who might have cashed it in. You don't have other nephews or nieces besides Mr. Isaiah Sommers who might have?"

Again her gaze turned to the wall. On an impulse, I asked her who the other boy was in the picture of Alderman Durham with her son.

"That's my nephew Colby. And no, you're not getting a shot along with the cops to pin something on him, nor yet on the alderman's Empower Youth Energy organization. Alderman Durham has been a good friend, to my family and to this neighborhood. And his group gives boys something to do with their time and energy."

It didn't seem like the right time or place to ask about the rumors that EYE members hustled campaign contributions with a judicious use of muscle. I turned back to the papers in front of us and asked about Rick Hoffman.

"What was he like? Can you imagine him stealing the policy from you?"

"Oh, what do I know about him? Except, like I said, his leather book that he ticked off our names in. He could have been Adolf Hitler for all I know."

"Did he sell insurance to a lot of people in this building?" I persisted.

"And why do you want to know that?"

"I'd like to find out if other people who bought from him had the same experience you did."

At that she finally looked at me, instead of through me. "In this building, no. At where Aaron—Mr. Sommers—worked, yes. My husband was at South Branch Scrap Metal. Mr. Hoffman knew people want to be buried decent, so he came around to places like that on the South Side, must have had ten or twenty businesses he'd hit on Friday afternoon. Sometimes he'd collect at the shop yard, sometimes he'd come here, it all depended on his schedule. And Aaron, Mr. Sommers, he paid his five dollars a week for fifteen years, until he was paid up."

"Would you have any way of knowing the names of some of the other people who bought from Hoffman?"

She studied me again, trying to assess whether this was a soft sell, and deciding finally to take a chance that I was being genuine. "I could give you four names, the men my husband worked with. They all bought from Hoffman because he made it easy, coming around like he did. Does this mean you understand I'm telling the truth about this?" She swept a hand toward my documents, still without looking at them.

I grimaced. "I have to consider all the possibilities, Ms. Sommers."

She eyed me bitterly. "I know my nephew meant it for the best, hiring you, but if he'd known how little respect you'd have—"

"I'm not disrespecting you, Ms. Sommers. You told your nephew you'd talk to me. You know the kinds of questions this must raise: there's a death certificate with your husband's name on it, with your name on it as the presenter, dated almost ten years ago, with a check made out to you through the Midway Insurance Agency. Someone cashed it. If I'm going to find out who, I have to start somewhere. It would help me believe you if I could find other people this same thing happened to."

Her face pinched up with anger, but after sitting in silence while the clock ticked off thirty seconds, she pulled a lined notepad from under the telephone. Wetting her index finger, she turned the pages of a weather-beaten address book and finally wrote down a series of names. Still without speaking, she handed the list to me.

The interview was over. I picked my way back along the unlit hall and down the stairs. The baby was still wailing. Outside, the men were still huddled over the Chevy.

When I unlocked the Mustang the men shouted over a jovial offer to trade. I grinned and waved. Oh, the kindness of strangers. It was only when people talked to me they got so hostile. There was a lesson in there for me, but not one I particularly wished to pursue.

It was almost three: I hadn't eaten since my yogurt at eight this morning. Maybe the situation would seem less depressing if I had some food. I passed a strip mall on my way to the expressway and bought a slice of cheese pizza. The crust was gooey, the surface glistened with oil, but I ate every bite with gusto. When I got out of my car at the office I realized I'd dripped oil down the front of my rose silk sweater. Warshawski zero, visitors five, at this point. At least I didn't have any business meetings this afternoon.

My part-time assistant, Mary Louise Neely, was at her desk. She handed me a packet with the video of the Radbuka interviews, which Beth Blacksin had messengered over. I stuffed it in my briefcase and brought Mary Louise up to date with the Sommers case, so she could check on the other men who had bought insurance from Rick Hoffman, then told her about Don's interest in Paul Radbuka.

"I couldn't find anyone named Radbuka in the system," I finished, "so either—"

"Vic—if he changed his name, he had to do so in front of a judge. There will be a court order." Mary Louise looked at me as though I were the village idiot.

I gaped at her like a dying pike and meekly went to turn on my computer. It was small comfort that if Radbuka or Ulrich or whatever his name was had taken any legal action, it wasn't in the system yet: I should have thought of that myself.

Mary Louise, not wanting to go stomping far and wide through the city, didn't believe Radbuka wasn't somewhere in the system. She did her own search and then said she would stop at the courts in the morning to double-check the paper record.

"Although maybe the therapist will tell you where to find him. What's her name?"

When I told her, her eyes opened wide. "Rhea Wiell? *The* Rhea Wiell?"

"You know her?" I spun around in my chair to face her.

"Not personally." Mary Louise's skin turned the same orangy pink as her hair. "But because, you know, because of my own story, I followed her career. I sat in on some of the trials where she testified."

Mary Louise had run away from an abusive home when she was a teenager. After a tumultuous ride through sex and drugs, she'd pulled herself together and become a police officer. In fact, the three children she was fostering had been rescued from an abusive home. So it wasn't surprising she paid special attention to a therapist who worked with molested children.

"Wiell used to be with the State Department of Children and Family Services. She was one of the staff therapists, she worked with kids, but she also was an expert witness in court cases that hinged on abuse. Remember the MacLean trial?"

As Mary Louise described it, the details began coming back to me. The guy was a law professor who'd started life as a Du Page County criminal prosecutor. When his name was put forward for a federal judgeship, his daughter, by then a grown woman, came forward to denounce him as having raped her when she was a child. She was insistent enough that she forced the state to bring charges.

Various right-wing family foundations had ridden to MacLean's rescue, claiming the daughter was the mouthpiece of a liberal smear campaign, since the father was a conservative Republican. In the end, the jury in the criminal sexual-assault trial found for the father, but his name was dropped from consideration for the judgeship.

"And Wiell testified?" I asked Mary Louise.

"More than that. She was the daughter's therapist. It was working with Rhea Wiell that made the woman recover the memories of abuse, when she'd blocked them for twenty years. The defense brought in Arnold Praeger from the Planted Memory Foundation.

He tried all kinds of cheap shots to make her look bad, but he couldn't shake her." Mary Louise glowed with admiration.

"So Praeger and Wiell go back a ways together."

"I don't know about that, but they definitely have been adversaries in court for quite a few years."

"I put in a search to ProQuest before I left this morning. If their fights have been in the news, I should have the stories." I brought up my ProQuest search. Mary Louise came to read over my shoulder. The case she had mentioned had generated a lot of ink at the time. I skimmed a couple of pieces in the *Herald-Star,* which praised Wiell's unflappable testimony.

Mary Louise bristled with anger over an op-ed piece Arnold Praeger had run in *The Wall Street Journal,* criticizing both Wiell and the law, which would allow the testimony of young children who had clearly been coached in what they remembered. Wiell wasn't even a reputable therapist, Praeger concluded. If she was, why had the State of Illinois dropped her from its payroll?

"Dropped her?" I said to Mary Louise, sending the piece to the printer with several of the others. "Do you know about that?"

"No. I assumed she decided private practice was a better place to be. Sooner or later, just about everyone gets burned out working for DCFS." Mary Louise's pale eyes were troubled. "I thought she was a really good, really genuine therapist. I can't believe the state would fire her, or at least not for any good reason. Maybe out of spite. She was the best they had, but there's always a lot of jealousy in offices like that. When I saw her in court, I used to imagine she was my mother. In fact, I was incredibly jealous of a woman I met who saw her professionally."

She laughed in embarrassment. "I've got to go, time for me to pick up the kids before class. I'll do those Sommers queries first thing tomorrow. You filling in your time sheets?"

"Yes, ma'am," I saluted her smartly.

"It's not a joke, Vic," she said sternly. "It's the only way—"

"I know, I know." Mary Louise doesn't like to be teased, which can be boring—but probably also is why she's such a good office manager.

When Mary Louise had left, promising to stop by the courts to check for Radbuka's change-of-name filing, I called a lawyer I knew in the State Department of Children and Family Services. We'd met at a seminar on women and law in the public sector and kept in touch in a desultory way.

She referred me to a supervisor in the DCFS office who would speak if it was far off the record. The supervisor wanted to call me back from a pay phone, in case her desk line was being monitored. I had to wait until five, when the woman stopped at a public phone in the basement of the Illinois Center on her way home. Before she'd tell me anything, my informant made me swear I wasn't calling on behalf of the Planted Memory Foundation.

"Not everyone at DCFS believes in hypnotherapy, but nobody here wants to see our clients hurt by one of those Planted Memory lawsuits."

When I assured her, by running through a list of possible references until I hit on a name she knew and trusted, she was amazingly frank. "Rhea was the most empathic therapist we ever used. She got incredible results from kids who would hardly even give their names to other therapists. I still miss her when we have certain kinds of trauma cases. The trouble was, she began to see herself as the priestess of DCFS. You couldn't question her results or her judgment.

"I don't remember exactly when she started her private practice, maybe six years ago, doing it part-time. But it was three years ago when we decided to sever her contract with the state. The press release said it was her decision, that she wanted to concentrate on her practice, but the feeling here was that she wouldn't take direction. She was always right; we—or the state attorney general, or anyone who disagreed with her—were wrong. And you can't have a staff person, someone you rely on with kids and in court, who always wants to be Joan of Arc."

"Did you think she might misrepresent a situation for her own glory?" I asked.

"Oh, no. Nothing like that. She wasn't out for glory—she was on a mission. I'm telling you, some of the younger women started calling her Mother Teresa, and not always out of admiration. Actually, that was part of the problem; she split the office straight in half between Rhea worshipers and Rhea doubters. And then she wouldn't let you question how she came to a conclusion. Like in that one case where the guy she was accusing of molestation was a former prosecutor who'd been nominated for a federal judgeship. Rhea wouldn't let us see her case notes before she testified. If the case had backfired, we could have been facing a ton of damages."

I thumbed through my stack of printouts. "Wasn't the daughter who brought the charges part of Wiell's private practice?"

"Yes, but Rhea was still on the state payroll, so the guy could have claimed she was using state office space or facilities for photocopying or whatnot—anything like that would have brought us into a lawsuit. We couldn't afford that kind of exposure. We had to let her go. Now you tell me, since I've been so frank with you, what's Rhea done that means a PI is interested in her?"

I'd known I'd have to cough up something. Tit for tat, it's how you keep information coming to you. "One of her clients was in the news this week. I don't know if you saw the guy with the recovered memories from the Holocaust? Someone wants to write a book about him and about how Rhea works. I've been asked to do some background checking."

"One thing Rhea knows better than any other therapist who ever worked for this office, and that's how to attract attention." My informant hung up smartly.

IX

Princess of Austria

So she is a legitimate therapist. Controversial but legitimate," I said to the glowing tip of Don's cigarette. "If you did a book with her, you wouldn't be signing on with a fraud."

"Actually, they're excited enough in New York that I went ahead and scheduled an appointment with the lady. Tomorrow at eleven. If you're free, want to sit in on it? Maybe she'll allow you to bring back a report to Dr. Herschel that will help you allay her concerns."

"Under the circumstances I can't imagine that happening. But I would like to meet Rhea Wiell."

We were sitting on Morrell's back porch. It was close to ten, but Morrell was still downtown at a meeting with some State Department officials—I had an uneasy feeling they were trying to persuade him to do some spying while he was in Kabul. I was wrapped in one of Morrell's old sweaters, drawing some small comfort from it—which made me feel like Mitch and Peppy—the dogs like to have my old socks to play with when I'm out of town. Lotty had brought my day to such a ragged end that I needed what comfort I could find.

I'd been running since I kissed Morrell good-bye this morning. Even though I still had a dozen urgent tasks, I was too tired to keep going. Before dictating my case notes, before calling Isaiah Sommers, before going home to run the dogs, before heading back to Morrell's place with a contract for Don Strzepek to cover my queries about Rhea Wiell, I needed to rest. Just half an hour on the portable bed in my back room, I'd thought. Half an hour would make me fit enough to cram another day's work into the evening. It was almost ninety minutes later that my client roused me.

"What made you go down to my aunt with all those accusations?" he demanded when the phone dragged me awake. "Couldn't you respect her widowhood?"

"What accusations?" My mouth and eyes felt as though they'd been stuffed with cotton.

"Going to her home and saying she stole money from the insurance company."

If I hadn't been bleary from my nap I might have answered more coolly. But maybe not.

"I will make every allowance for your aunt's grief, but that is not what I said. And before you call to accuse me of such abominable behavior, why don't you ask me what I said."

"All right. I'm asking you." His voice was leaden with suppressed anger.

"I showed your aunt the canceled check the company issued when a death claim was submitted nine years ago. I asked her what she knew about it. That is not an accusation. A check for her had been made out in care of the Midway Insurance Agency. I couldn't pretend her name wasn't on the check. I couldn't pretend Ajax hadn't issued it based on a bona fide death certificate. I had to ask her about it."

"You should have talked to me first. I'm the person who paid you."

"I cannot consult with clients about every step I take in an investigation. I'd never get anything done."

"You took my money. You spent it on accusing my aunt. Your contract says I can terminate our arrangement at any time. I am terminating it now."

"Fine," I snapped. "Terminate away. Someone committed fraud with your uncle's policy. If you want them to get away with it, so be it."

"Of course I don't want that, but I'll look into the matter on my own, in a way that will respect my aunt. I should have known a white detective would act just like the police. I should have listened to my wife." He hung up.

It wasn't the first time an angry client had fired me, but I've never learned to take it with equanimity. I could have done things differently. I should have called him, called him before I went to see his aunt, gotten him on my side. Or at least called him before I went to sleep. I could have kept my temper—my besetting sin.

I tried to remember exactly what I'd said to his aunt. Damn it, I should do as Mary Louise said, dictate my notes as soon as I finished a meeting. Better late than never: I could start with my phone conversation with the client. Ex-client. I dialed up the word-processing service I use and dictated a summary of the call, adding a letter to Sommers confirming that he'd canceled my services; I'd enclose his uncle's policy with the letter. When I'd finished with Isaiah Sommers, I dictated notes from my other conversations of the day, working backward from my informant at Family Services to my meeting with Ralph at Ajax.

Lotty called on the other line when I was halfway through reconstructing my encounter with the insurance agent Howard Fepple. "Max told me about the program he saw with you at Morrell's last night," she said, without preamble. "It sounded very disturbing."

"It was."

"He didn't know whether to believe the man's story or not. Did Morrell make a tape of the interview?"

"Not that I know of. I got a copy of the tape today, which I can—"

"I want to see it. Will you bring it to my apartment this evening, please." It came out as a command, not a request.

"Lotty, this isn't your operating room. I don't have time to stop at your place tonight, but in the morning I—"

"This is a very simple favor, Victoria, which has nothing to do with my operating room. You don't need to leave the tape with me, but I want to see it. You can stand over me while I watch it."

"Lotty, I don't have the time. I will get copies made tomorrow and let you have one of your very own. But this one is for a client who hired me to investigate the situation."

"A client?" She was outraged. "Did Max hire you without either of you talking to me?"

My forehead felt as though it were squeezed inside a vise. "If he did, that's between him and me, not you and me. What difference does it make to you?"

"What difference? That he violated a trust, that's what it matters. When he told me about this person at the conference, this man calling himself Radbuka, I said we shouldn't act hastily and that I would give him my opinion after I had seen the interview."

I took a deep breath and tried to bring my brain into focus. "So the Radbuka name means something to you."

"And to Max. And to Carl. From our days in London. Max thought we should hire you to find out about this man. I wanted to wait. I thought Max respected my opinion."

She was almost spitting mad, but her explanation made me say gently, "Take it easy, Lotty. Max didn't hire me. This is a separate matter."

I told her about Don Strzepek's interest in doing a book about Rhea Wiell, showcasing Paul Radbuka's recovered memory. "I'm sure he wouldn't object to sharing the tape with you, but I really don't have time to do it tonight. I still need to finish some work here, go to my own place to look after the dogs, and then I'm going up to Evanston. Do you want me to tell Morrell that you'll be coming up to view the tape at his place?"

"I want the dead past to bury the dead," she burst out. "Why are you letting this Don go digging around in it?"

"I'm not letting him, and I'm not stopping him. All I'm doing is checking to see whether Rhea Wiell is a genuine therapist."

"Then you're letting, not stopping."

She sounded close to tears. I picked my words carefully. "I can only begin to imagine how painful it must be to you to be reminded of the war years, but not everyone feels that way."

"Yes, to many people it is a game. Something to romanticize or kitschify or use for titillation. And a book about a ghoul feasting on the remains of the dead only helps make that happen."

"If Paul Radbuka is not a ghoul but has a genuine past in the concentration camp he mentioned, then he has a right to claim his heritage. What does the person in your group who's connected to the Radbukas say about this? Did you talk to him? Or her?"

"That person no longer exists," she said harshly. "This is between Max and Carl and me. And now you. And now this journalist, Don whoever he is. And the therapist. And every jackal in New York and Hollywood who will pick over the bones and salivate with pleasure at another shocking tale. Publishers and movie studios make fortunes from titillating the comfortable well-fed middle class of Europe and America with tales of torture."

I had never heard Lotty speak in such a bitter way. It hurt, as if my fingers were being run through a grater. I didn't know what to say, except to repeat my offer to bring her a copy of the tape the next day. She hung up on me.

I sat at my desk a long time, blinking back tears of my own. My arms ached. I lacked the will to move or act in any meaningful way, but in the end, I picked up the phone and continued dictating my notes to the word-processing center. When I had finished that, I got up slowly, like an invalid, and printed out a copy of my contract for Don Strzepek.

"Maybe if I talked to Dr. Herschel myself," Don said now, as we sat on Morrell's porch. "She's imagining me as a TV reporter sticking a mike in front of her face after her family's been destroyed. She's right in a way, about how we comfortable Americans and Europeans like to titillate ourselves with tales of torture. I shall have to keep that thought in mind as a corrective when I'm working on this book. All the same, maybe I can persuade her that I also have some capacity for empathy."

"Maybe. Max will probably let me bring you to his dinner party on Sunday; at least you could meet Lotty in an informal way."

I didn't really see it, though. Usually, when Lotty got on her high horse, Max would snort and say she was in her "Princess of Austria" mode. That would spark another flare from her, but she'd back away from her more extreme demands. Tonight's outburst had been rawer than that—not the disdain of a Hapsburg princess, but a ragged fury born of grief.

Lotty Herschel's Story:

Four Gold Coins

My mother was seven months pregnant and weak from hunger, so my father took Hugo and me to the train. It was early in the morning, still dark, in fact: we Jews were trying not to attract any more attention than necessary. Although we had permits to leave, all our documents, the tickets, we could still be stopped at any second. I wasn't yet ten and Hugo only five, but we knew the danger so well we didn't need Papa's command to be silent in the streets.

Saying good-bye to my mother and Oma had frightened me. My mother used to spend weeks away from us with Papa, but I had never left Oma before. By then of course everyone was living together in a little flat in the Leopoldsgasse—I can't remember how many aunts and cousins now, besides my grandparents—but at least twenty.

In London, lying in the cold room at the top of the house, on the narrow iron bed Minna considered appropriate for a child, I wouldn't think about the cramped space on the Leopoldsgasse. I concentrated on remembering Oma and Opa's beautiful flat where I had my own white lacy bed, the curtains at the window dotted with rosebuds. My school, where my friend Klara and I were always one and two in the class. How hurt I was—I couldn't understand why she stopped playing with me and then why I had to leave the school altogether.

I had whined at first over sharing a room with six other cousins in a place with peeling paint, but Papa took me for a walk early one morning so he could talk to me alone about our changed circumstances. He was never cruel, not like Uncle Arthur, Mama's brother who actually beat Aunt Freia, besides hitting his own children.

We walked along the canal as the sun was rising and Papa explained how hard things were for everyone, for Oma and Opa, forced out of the family flat after all these years, and for Mama, with all her pretty jewels stolen by the Nazis and worrying about how her children would be fed and clothed, let alone educated. "Lottchen, you are the big girl in the family now. Your cheerful spirit is Mama's most precious gift. Show her you are the brave one, the cheerful one, and now that she's sick with the new baby coming, show her you can help her by not complaining and by taking care of Hugo."

What shocks me now is knowing that my father's parents were also in that flat and how little I remember of them. In fact, I'm pretty sure that it was their flat. They were foreign, you see, from Belarus: they were part of the vast throng of Eastern European Jews who had flocked into Vienna around the time of the First World War.

Oma and Opa looked down on them. It confuses me, that realization, because I loved my mother's parents so much. They doted on me, too: I was their precious Lingerl's beloved child. But I think Oma and Opa despised Papa's parents, for speaking only Yiddish, not German, and for their odd clothes and religious practices.

It was a terrible humiliation for Oma and Opa, when they were forced to leave the Renngasse to live in that immigrant Jewish quarter. People used to call it the Matzoinsel, the matzo island, a term of contempt. Even Oma and Opa, when they didn't think Papa was around, would talk about his family on the Insel. Oma would laugh her ladylike laugh at the fact that Papa's mother wore a wig, and I felt guilty, because I was the one who had revealed this primitive practice to Oma. She liked to interrogate me about the "customs on the Insel" after I had been there, and then she would remind me that I was a Herschel, I was to stand up straight and make something of my life. And not to use the Yiddish I picked up on the Insel; that was vulgar and Herschels were never vulgar.

Papa would take me to visit his parents once a month or so. I was supposed to call them Zeyde and Bobe, Grandpa and Grandma in Yiddish, as Opa and Oma are in German. When I think about them now I grow hot with shame, for withholding from them the affection and respect they desired: Papa was their only son, I was the oldest grandchild. But even to call them Zeyde and Bobe, as they requested, seemed disgusting to me. And Bobe's blond wig over her close-cropped black hair, that seemed disgusting as well.

I hated that I looked like Papa's side of the family. My mother was so lovely, very fair, with beautiful curls and a mischievous smile. And as you can see, I am dark, and not at all beautiful. *Mischlinge*, cousin Minna called me, half-breed, although never in front of my grandparents: to Opa and Oma I was always beautiful, because I was their darling Lingerl's daughter. It wasn't until I came to live with Minna in England that I ever felt ugly.

What torments me is that I can't recall my father's sisters or their children at all. I shared a bed with five or maybe six cousins, and I can't remember them, only that I hated not being in my own lovely white bedroom by myself. I remember kissing Oma and weeping, but I didn't even say good-bye to Bobe.

You think I should remember I was only a child? No. Even a child has the capacity for human and humane behavior.

Each child was allowed one small suitcase for the train. Oma wanted us to take leather valises from her own luggage—those had not been of interest to the Nazis when they stole her silver and her jewels. But Opa was more practical and understood Hugo and I mustn't attract attention by looking as though we came from a rich home. He found us cheap cardboard cases, which anyway were easier for young children to carry.

By the day the train left, Hugo and I had packed and repacked our few possessions many times, trying to decide what we couldn't bear to live without. The night before we left, Opa took the dress I was going to wear on the train out to Oma. Everyone was asleep, except me: I was lying rigid with nervousness in the bed I shared with the other cousins. When Opa came in I watched him through slits in my closed eyes. When he tiptoed out with the dress, I slid out of bed and followed him to my grandmother's side. Oma put a finger on her lips when she saw me and silently picked apart the waistband. She took four gold coins from the hem of her own skirt and stitched them into the waist, underneath the buttons.

"These are your security," Opa said. "Tell no one, not Hugo, not Papa, not anyone. You won't know when you will need them." He and Oma didn't want to cause friction in the family by letting them know they had a small emergency hoard. If the aunts and uncles knew Lingerl's children were getting four precious gold coins—well, when people are frightened and living too close together, anything can happen.

The next thing I knew Papa was shaking me awake, giving me a cup of the weak tea we all drank for breakfast. Some adult had found enough canned milk for each child to get a tablespoon in it most mornings.

If I had realized I wouldn't see any of them again—but it was hard enough to leave, to go to a strange country where we knew only cousin Minna, and only that she was a bitter woman who made all the children uncomfortable when she came to Kleinsee for her three-week holiday in the summers—if I'd known it was the last good-bye I wouldn't have been able to bear—the leaving, or the next several years.

When the train left it was a cold April day, rain pouring in sheets across the Leopoldsgasse as we walked—not to the central station but a small suburban one that wouldn't attract attention. Papa wore a long red scarf, which he put on so Hugo and I could spot him easily from the train. He was a café violinist, or had been, anyway, and when he saw us leaning out a window, he whipped out his violin and tried to play one of the Gypsy tunes he had taught us to dance to. Even Hugo could tell misery was making his hand quaver, and he howled at Papa to stop making such a noise.

"I will see you very soon," Papa assured us. "Lottchen, you will find someone who needs a willing worker. I can do anything, remember that—wait tables, haul wood or coal, play in a hotel orchestra."

As the train pulled away I held the back of Hugo's jacket and the two of us leaned out the window with all the other children, waving until Papa's red scarf had turned to an invisible speck in our own eyes.

We had the usual fears all Kindertransport children report as we traveled through Austria and Germany, of the guards who tried to frighten us, of the searches through our luggage, standing very still while they looked for any valuables: we were allowed a single ten-mark piece each. I thought my heart would be visible through my dress, it was beating so hard, but they didn't feel my clothes, and the gold coins traveled with me safely. And then we passed out of Germany into Holland, and for the first time since the Anschluss we were suddenly surrounded by warm and welcoming adults, who showered us with bread and meat and chocolates.

I don't remember much of the crossing. We had a calm sea, I think, but I was so nervous that my stomach was twisted in knots even without any serious waves. When we landed we looked around anxiously for Minna in the crowd of adults who had come to meet the boat, but all the children were claimed and we were left standing on the dock. Finally a woman from the refugee committee showed up: Minna had left instructions for us to be sent on to London by train, but she had delayed getting word to the refugee committee until that morning. We spent the night in the camp at Hove with the other children who had no sponsors, and went on to London in the morning. When we got to the station, to Liverpool Street—it was massive, we clung to each other while engines belched and loudspeakers bellowed incomprehensible syllables and people brushed past us on important missions. I clutched Hugo's hand tightly.

Cousin Minna had sent a workman to fetch us, giving him a photograph against which he anxiously studied our faces. He spoke English, which we didn't understand at all, or Yiddish, which we didn't understand well, but he was pleasant, bustling us into a cab, pointing out the Thames as we rolled over it, the Houses of Parliament and Big Ben, giving us each a bit of queer paste-filled sandwich in case we were hungry after our long trip.

It was only when we got to that narrow old house in the north of London that we found out Minna would take me and not Hugo. The man from the factory settled us in a forbidding front room, where we sat without moving, so fearful we were of making a noise or being a nuisance. After some very long time, Minna swept in from work, full of anger, and announced that Hugo was to go on, that the foreman from the glove factory would be coming for him in an hour.

"One child and one child only. I told her highness Madame Butterfly that when she wrote begging for my charity. She may choose to roll around in the hay with a Gypsy but that doesn't mean the rest of us have to look after her children."

I tried to protest, but she said she could throw me out on the street. "Better be grateful to me, you little mongrels. I spent all day persuading the foreman to take Hugo instead of sending him to the child welfare authorities."

The foreman, Mr. Nussbaum his name was, actually turned out to be a good foster father to Hugo; he even set him up in business many years later. But you can only guess how the two of us felt that day when he arrived to take Hugo away with him: the last sight either of us had then of any familiar face of our childhood.

Like the Nazi guards, Minna searched my clothes for valuables: she refused to believe the penury to which the family was reduced. Fortunately, my Oma had been clever enough to evade both Nazis and Minna. Those gold coins helped pay my fees in medical school, but that was a long way ahead, in a future I didn't imagine as I sobbed for my parents and my brother.

X

In the Mind Reader's Lair

When I finally woke the next morning, my head was heavy with the detritus of dreams and difficult sleep. I once read that a year or eighteen months after losing them, you dream of your dead as they were in their prime. I suppose I must sometimes dream of my mother as she was in my childhood, vivid and intense, but last night she was dying, eyes heavy with morphine, face unrecognizable as disease had leached flesh from bone. Lotty and my mother are such intertwined strands in my mind that it was almost inevitable that her distress would overlay my sleep.

Morrell looked at me questioningly when I sat up. He had come in after I went to bed, but I was tossing, not sleeping. His impending departure made him feverishly nervous; we made love with a kind of frantic unsatisfying energy but fell asleep without talking. In the morning light he traced my cheekbones with his finger and asked if it was his leaving that had disturbed my sleep.

I gave a twisted smile. "My own stuff this time." I gave him a brief synopsis of the previous day.

"Why don't we go to Michigan for the weekend?" he said. "We both need a breather. You can't do anything on a Saturday, anyway, and we can give each other better comfort away from all these people. I love Don like a brother, but having him here right now is a bit much. We'll come back in time for Michael and Carl's concert on Sunday."

My muscles unknotted at the thought, and it sent me into the day with better energy than my tormented night warranted. After stopping at home to take the dogs for a swim, I drove into the West Loop to the Unblinking Eye, the camera and video place I use when only the best will do. I explained what I wanted to Maurice Redken, the technician I usually work with.

We ran my copy of the Channel 13 video through one of their machines, watching Radbuka's naked face as he went through the torments of his life. When he said, "My Miriam, where is my Miriam? I want my Miriam," the camera was right in his face. I froze the image there and asked Maurice to make prints of that and a couple of other close-ups for me. I was hoping Rhea Wiell would introduce me to Radbuka, but if she didn't, the stills would help Mary Louise and me track him down.

Maurice promised to have both the stills and three copies of the tape ready for me by the day's end. It wasn't quite ten-thirty when we finished. There wasn't time for me to go to my office before Don's appointment with Rhea Wiell, but I could walk the two miles from the Eye to Water Tower if I didn't dawdle—I hate paying Gold Coast parking fees.

Water Tower Place is a shopping mecca on North Michigan, a favorite drop-off place for tour buses from small Midwestern towns as well as an oasis for local teens. Threading my way through girls whose pierced navels showed below their cropped T-shirts and women pushing expensive baby buggies overflowing with packages, I found Don leaning against the back entrance. He was so engrossed in his book he didn't look up when I stopped next to him. I squinted to read the spine: *Hypnotic Induction and Suggestion: an Introductory Manual.*

"Does this tell you how Ms. Wiell does it?" I asked.

He blinked and closed the book. "It tells me that blocked memories really can be accessed through hypnosis. Or at least the authors claim so. Fortunately I only have to see if Wiell has a sellable book in her, not sort out whether her therapy is legitimate. I'm going to introduce you as an investigator who may help collect background data if Wiell and the publisher come to terms. You can say anything you like."

He looked at his watch and fished a cigarette from his breast pocket. Although he'd changed clothes, into a pressed open-necked shirt and a tweed jacket, he still looked half-asleep. I took the book on hypnotic induction while Don lit his cigarette. Broadly speaking, hypnosis seemed to be used in two main ways: suggestive hypnosis helped people break bad habits, and insight or exploratory hypnosis helped them understand themselves better. Recovering memories was only one small part of using hypnosis in therapy.

Don pinched off the glowing end of his cigarette and put the stub back in his pocket. "Time to go, Ms. Warshawski."

I followed him into the building. "This book could help you end that expensive habit for good."

He stuck out his tongue at me. "I wouldn't know what to do with my hands if I quit."

We went behind a newsstand on the ground floor, in a dark alcove which held the elevators to the office floor. It wasn't exactly secret, just out of the way enough to keep the shopping hordes from straying there by mistake. I studied the tenant board. Plastic surgeons, endodontists, beauty salons, even a synagogue. What an odd combination.

"I called over to the Jane Addams School, as you suggested," Don said abruptly when we were alone on an elevator. "First I couldn't find anyone who knew Wiell—she did her degree fifteen years ago. But when I started talking about the hypnotherapy, the department secretary remembered. Wiell was married then, used her husband's name."

We got off the elevator and found ourselves at a point where four long corridors came together. "What did they think of her at UIC?" I asked.

He looked at his appointment book. "I think we go right here. There's some jealousy—a suggestion she was a charlatan, but when I pushed it seemed to stem from the fact that social work had made her rich—doesn't happen to too many people, I gather."

We stopped in front of a blond door with Wiell's name and professional initials painted on it. I felt a tingle from the idea that this woman might read my mind. She might know me better than I knew myself. Was that where hypnotic suggestibility got its start? The urgent desire to be understood so intimately?

Don pushed the door open. We were in a tiny vestibule with two shut doors and a third one that was open. This led to a waiting room, where a sign invited us to sit down and relax. It added that all cell phones and pagers should be turned off. Don and I obediently pulled out our phones. He switched his off, but mine had run down again without my noticing.

The waiting room was decorated with such attention to comfort that it even held a carafe of hot water and a selection of herbal teas. New Age music tinkled softly; padded chairs faced a four-foot-high fish tank built into the far wall. The fish seemed to rise and fall in time to the music.

"What do you think this setup costs?" Don was trying the other two doors. One turned out to be a bathroom; the other was locked.

"I don't know—installing it took a bundle, but looking after it wouldn't take too much. Except for the rent, of course. The nicotine in your system is keeping you awake. These fish are putting me to sleep."

He grinned. "You're going to sleep, Vic: when you wake up—"

"It isn't like that, although people are always nervous at first and imagine the television version." The locked door had opened and Rhea Wiell appeared behind us. "You're from the publishing company, aren't you?"

She seemed smaller in person than she had on television, but her face held the same serenity I'd noticed on screen. She was dressed as she had been on camera, in soft clothes that flowed like an Indian mystic's.

Don shook her hand, unembarrassed, and introduced both of us. "If you and I decide to work together, Vic may help with some of the background checking."

Wiell stood back to let us pass in front of her into her office. It, too, was designed to put us at ease, with a reclining chair, a couch, and her own office chair all covered in soft green. Her diplomas hung behind her desk: the MSW from the Jane Addams School of Social Work, a certificate from the American Institute of Clinical Hypnosis, and her Illinois license as a psychiatric social worker.

I perched on the edge of the recliner while Don took the couch. Wiell sat in her office chair, her hands loosely crossed in her lap. She looked like Jean Simmons in *Elmer Gantry*.

"When we saw you on Channel Thirteen the other night, I immediately realized you had a very powerful story to tell, you and Paul Radbuka," Don said. "You must have thought about putting it into a book before I called, hadn't you?"

Wiell smiled faintly. "Of course I've wanted to: if you saw the whole program, then you're aware that my work is—misunderstood—in a number of circles. A book validating the recovery of blocked trauma would be enormously useful. And Paul Radbuka's story would be unusual enough—powerful enough—to force people to pay serious attention to the issue."

Don leaned forward, chin on his clasped hands. "I'm new to the subject—my first exposure came two nights ago. I've been cram-ming hard, reading a manual on hypnotic suggestion, looking at articles about you, but I'm definitely not up to speed."

She nodded. "Hypnosis is only one part of a total therapeutic approach, and it's controversial because it isn't understood very well. The field of memory, what we remember, how we remember, and maybe most interestingly why we remember—none of that is really known right now. The research seems exciting to me, but I'm not a scientist and I don't pretend to have the time to follow experimental work in depth."

"Would your book focus exclusively on Paul Radbuka?" I asked.

"Since Don—I hope you don't mind my using your first name?— Don called yesterday, I've been thinking it over; I believe I should use some other case histories, as well, to show that my work with Paul isn't—well, the kind of fly-by-night treatment that Planted Memory therapists like to claim."

"What do you see as the book's central point?" Don patted his jacket pocket reflexively, then pulled out a pen in lieu of his half-smoked cigarette.

"To show that our memories are reliable. To show the difference between planted memories and genuine ones. I began going through my patient files last night after I finished work and found several people whose histories would make this point quite strongly. Three had complete amnesia about their childhoods when they started therapy. One had partial memories, and two had what they thought were continuous memories, although therapy unlocked new insights for them. In some ways it's most exciting to uncover memories for someone who has amnesia, but the harder work is verifying, filling in gaps for people who have some recall."

Don interrupted to ask if there was some way to verify memories that were uncovered in treatment. I expected Wiell to become defensive, but she responded quite calmly.

"That's why I earmarked these particular cases. For each of them there is at least one other person, a witness to their childhood, who can corroborate what came up in here. For some it's a brother or sister. In one case it's a social worker; for two, there are primary-school teachers."

"We'd have to get written permission." Don was making notes. "For the patients and for their verifiers. Witnesses."

She nodded again. "Of course their real identities would be carefully concealed, not just to protect themselves but to protect family members and colleagues who could be harmed by such narratives. But, yes, we'll get written permission."

"Are these other patients also Holocaust survivors?" I ventured.

"Helping Paul was an incredible privilege." A smile lit her face with a kind of ecstatic joy, so intense, so personal, that I instinctively shrank back on the recliner away from her. "Most of my clients are dealing with terrible traumas, to be sure, but within the context of this culture. To get Paul to that point, to the point of being a little boy speaking broken German with his helpless playmates in a concentration camp, was the most powerful experience of my life. I don't even know how we can do it justice in print." She looked at her hands, adding in a choked voice, "I think he's recently recovered a fragment of memory of witnessing his mother's death."

"I'll do my best for you," Don muttered. He, too, had shifted away from her.

"You said you'd be concealing people's real identities," I said. "So is Paul Radbuka not his real name?"

The ecstasy left Wiell's face, replaced again by her patina of professional calm. "He's the one person who doesn't seem to have any living family left to be upset by his revelations. Besides, he's so intensely proud of his newly recovered identity that it would be impossible to persuade him to use a cover name."

"So you've discussed it with him?" Don asked eagerly. "He's willing to take part?"

"I haven't had time to talk about it with any of my patients." She smiled faintly. "You only broached the idea yesterday, after all. But I know how intensely Paul feels: it's why he insisted on speaking up at the Birnbaum conference earlier this week. I think, too, he'd do anything he could to support my work, because it's changed his life so dramatically."

"How did he come to remember the name Radbuka?" I said. "If he was raised by this foster father from the age of four and wrenched from his birth family in infancy—have I got that chronology right?"

Wiell shook her head at me. "I hope your role isn't to try to set traps for me, Ms. Warshawski. If it is, I'll have to look for a different publisher than Envision Press. Paul found some papers in his father's desk—his foster father, I should say—and they pointed the way to his birth name for him."

"I wasn't trying to set a trap, Ms. Wiell. But it would certainly strengthen the book if we could get some outside corroboration of his Radbuka identity. And it's remotely possible that I am in a position to provide that. To be candid, I have friends who came to England from central Europe with the Kindertransport in the last months before the war began. Apparently one of their group of special friends in London was named Radbuka. If it turns out your client is a relation, it might mean a great deal, both to him and to my friends who lost so many family members."

Again the rapturous smile swept across her face. "Ah, if you can introduce him to his relatives, that would be an indescribable gift to Paul. Who are these people? Do they live in England? How do you know them?"

"I know two of them who live here in Chicago; the third is a musician who's visiting from London for a few days. If I could talk to your client—"

"Not until I've consulted with him," she cut me off. "And I would have to have your—friends'—names before I could do so. I hate to have to be so suspicious, but I have had too many traps set for me by the Planted Memory Foundation."

My eyes narrowed as I tried to hear behind her words. Was this paranoia born of too much skirmishing with Arnold Praeger, or a legitimate prudence?

Before I could decide, Don said, "You don't think Max would mind your giving his name, do you, Vic?"

"Max?" Wiell cried. "Max Loewenthal?"

"How do you know him?" Don asked, again before I could respond.

"He spoke at the session on the efforts of survivors to track down the fates of their families and whether they had any assets tied up in Swiss or German banks. Paul and I sat in on that: we hoped we could learn some new ideas for ways of looking for his family. If Max is your friend, I'm sure Paul would be glad to talk to him—he seemed an extraordinary man, gentle, empathic, yet assured, authoritative."

"That's a good description of his personality," I said, "but he also has a strong sense of privacy. He would be most annoyed if Paul Radbuka approached him without my having a chance to speak to Mr. Radbuka first."

"You can rest assured that I understand the value of privacy. My relations with my clients would not be possible if I didn't protect them." Wiell gave me the same sweet, steely smile she'd directed at Arnold Praeger on TV the other night.

"So can we arrange a meeting with your client, where I can talk to him before introducing him to my friends?" I tried to keep irritation out of my voice, but I knew I couldn't match her in sanctity.

"Before I do anything, I will have to talk to Paul. Surely you understand that any other course would violate my relationship with him." She wrote Max's name in her datebook next to Paul Radbuka's appointment: her square, printlike hand was easy to read upside down.

"Of course I understand that," I said with what patience I could muster. "But I can't let Paul Radbuka come to Mr. Loewenthal out of the blue in the belief that they're related. In fact, I don't think Mr. Loewenthal is himself a part of the Radbuka family. If I could ask Paul a few questions first, it might spare everyone some anxiety."

She shook her head with finality: she would not turn Paul over to someone like me, an unskilled outsider. "Whether it's Mr. Loewenthal or his musician friend who is part of the family, I assure you, I would approach them with the utmost empathy. And the first step is to talk to Paul, to get his permission for me to go to them. How long will your musician be in Chicago?"

At this point I didn't want to tell her anything about anyone I knew, but Don said, "I think he said that he's leaving for the West Coast on Monday."

While I fumed to myself, Don got Wiell to give a précis on how hypnosis worked and how she used it—sparingly, and only after her patients felt able to trust her—before he brought up the kind of controversy the book was likely to generate.

He grinned engagingly. "From our standpoint, controversy is highly desirable, because it gives a book access to the kind of press coverage you can't buy. But from yours—you may not want that kind of spotlight on you and your practice."

She smiled back at him. "Like you, I would welcome the publicity—although for a different reason. I want as many people as possible to start understanding how we block memories, how we recover them, and how we can become liberated in the process. The Planted Memory Foundation has done a great deal of damage to people suffering from trauma. I haven't had the resources to make the truth clear to a wider audience. This book would help me greatly."

A silvery bell, like a Japanese temple bell, chimed on her desk. "We'll have to stop now—I have another patient coming and I need time to prepare for my session."

I handed her my card, reminding her that I wanted an early meeting with Paul Radbuka. She shook my hand in a cool, dry clasp, giving my hand a slight pressure intended to reassure me of her goodwill. To Don she added that she could help him stop smoking if he wanted.

"Most of my hypnotic work is in the arena of self-exploration, but I do work with habit management sometimes."

Don laughed. "I hope we'll be working closely together for the next year or so. If I decide I'm ready to quit we'll put the manuscript aside while I lie back on your couch here."

XI

Ramping Up

As we walked past the liposuckers to the elevator, Don congratulated himself on how well things had gone. "I'm a believer: it's going to be a great project. Those eyes of hers could convince me to do just about anything."

"They apparently did," I said dryly. "I wish you hadn't brought Max's name into the discussion."

"Chrissake, Vic, it was a pure fluke that she guessed it was Max Loewenthal." He stood back as the elevator doors opened to let out an elderly couple. "This is going to be a career-saving book for me. I bet I can get my agent to go to high six figures, not to mention the film rights—don't you see Dustin Hoffman as the broken-down Radbuka remembering his past?"

Lotty's bitter remark on ghouls profiting on the remains of the dead came back to me full force. "You said you wanted to prove to Lotty Herschel that you're not the mike-in-the-face kind of journalist. She's not going to be very persuaded if you're prancing around in glee about turning her friends' misery into commercial movies."

"Vic, get a grip," Don said. "Can't you let me have my moment of triumph? Of course I won't violate Dr. Herschel's most sacred feelings. I started out feeling a bit doubtful of Rhea, but by the end of the hour she had me totally on her side—sorry if the excitement's gone to my head."

"She rubbed me the wrong way a bit," I said.

"That's because she wouldn't toss you her patient's home phone number. Which she absolutely should not give anyone. You know that."

"I know that," I had to agree. "I guess what bugs me is her wanting to mastermind the situation: she'll meet Max and Lotty and Carl, she'll decide what they're about, but she's resisting the idea that I might meet her client. Don't you think it's odd that he gave her office as his home address—as if his identity was wrapped up in her?"

"You're overreacting, Vic, because you like to be the one in control yourself. You read some of the articles you printed out for me on the attacks against her by Planted Memory, right? She's sensible to be cautious."

He paused while the elevator landed and we negotiated our way past the group waiting to get on. I scanned them, hoping I might see Paul Radbuka, wondering about the destination of the people boarding. Were they getting fat sucked out? Root canals? Which one was Rhea Wiell's next patient?

Don continued with the thought uppermost in his own mind. "Do you think it's Lotty, Max, or Carl who really is related to Radbuka? They sound pretty prickly for people who are only looking out for their friends' interests."

I stopped behind the newsstand to stare at him. "I don't think any of them is related to Radbuka. That's why I'm so annoyed that Ms. Wiell has Max's name now. I know, I know," I added, as he started to interrupt, "you didn't really give it to her. But she's so focused on her prize exhibit's well-being that she's not thinking outside that landscape now to anyone else's needs."

"But why should she?" he asked. "I mean, I understand that you want her to be as empathic to Max or Dr. Herschel as she is to Paul Radbuka, but how could she be that concerned about a group of strangers? Besides, she's got such an exciting event going on with what she's done with this guy that it's not surprising, really. But why are your friends so very defensive if it isn't their own family they're worrying about?"

"Good grief, Don—you're almost as experienced as Morrell in writing about war-scarred refugees. I'm sure you can imagine how it must have felt, to be in London with a group of children who all shared the same traumas—first of leaving their families behind to go to a strange country with a strange language, then the even bigger trauma of the horrific way in which their families died. I think you'd feel a sense of bonding that went beyond friendship—everyone's experiences would seem as though they had happened to you person-ally."

"I suppose you're right. Of course you are. I only want to get in with Rhea on the story of the decade." He grinned again, disarming me, and pulled the half-smoked cigarette out of his pocket again. "Until I decide to let Rhea cure me, I need to get this inside me. Can you come over to the Ritz with me? Share a glass of champagne and let me feel just a minute moment of euphoria about my project?"

I still wasn't in a very celebratory mood. "Let me check with my answering service while you go over to the hotel. Then a quick one, I guess."

I went back to the corner to use the pay phones, since my cell phone was dead. Why couldn't I let Don have his moment of tri-umph, as he had put it? Was he right, that I was only resentful be-cause Rhea Wiell wouldn't give me Radbuka's phone number? But that sense of an ecstatic vision when she was talking about her tri-umph with Paul Radbuka had made me uncomfortable. It was the ecstasy of a votary, though, not the triumphant smirk of a charla-tan, so why should I let it raise my hackles?

I fed change into the phone and dialed my answering service.

"Vic! Where have you been?" Christie Weddington, a day opera-tor who'd been with the service for longer than me, jolted me back to my own affairs.

"What's up?"

"Beth Blacksin has phoned three times, wanting a comment; Murray Ryerson has called twice, besides messages from a whole bunch of other reporters." She read off a string of names and num-bers. "Mary Louise, she called and said she was switching the office line over to us because she felt like she was under siege."

"But about what?"

"I don't know, Vic, I just take the messages. Murray said some-thing about Alderman Durham, though, and—here it is." She read the message in a flat, uninflected voice. " 'Call me and tell me what's going on with Bull Durham. Since when have you started robbing the widow and orphan of their mite?' "

I was completely bewildered. "I guess just forward all those to my office computer. Are there any business messages, things that don't come from reporters?"

I could hear her clicking through her screen. "I don't think—oh, here is something from a Mr. Devereux at Ajax." She read me Ralph's number.

I tried Murray first. He's an investigative reporter with the *Herald-*

Star who does occasional special reports for Channel 13. This was the first time he'd called me in some months—we'd had quite a falling out over a case that had involved the *Star*'s owners. In the end, we'd made a kind of fragile peace, but we've been avoiding involvement with each other's cases.

"Warshawski, what in hell did you do to yank Bull Durham's chain so hard?"

"Hi, Murray. Yes, I'm depressed about the Cubs and worried because Morrell is leaving for Kabul in a few days. But otherwise things go on same as always. How about you?"

He paused briefly, then snarled at me not to be a smart-mouthed pain in the ass.

"Why don't you start from the beginning?" I suggested. "I've been in meetings all morning and have no idea what our aldercreatures have been saying or doing."

"Bull Durham is leading a charge of pickets outside the Ajax company headquarters."

"Oh—on the slave-reparations issue?"

"Right. Ajax is his first target. His handouts name you as an agent of the company involved in the continuing suppression of black policyholders by depriving them of their settlements."

"I see." A recorded message interrupted us, telling me to deposit twenty-five cents if I wanted to continue the call. "Gotta go, Murray, I'm out of change."

I hung up on his squawk that that was hardly an answer—what had I *done*?! That must be why Ralph Devereux was calling. To find out what I'd done to provoke a full-scale picket. What a mess. When my client—ex-client—told me he was going to take steps, these must have been the ones he had in mind. I gritted my teeth and put another thirty-five cents into the phone.

I got Ralph's secretary, but by the time she put me through to him I'd been on hold so long I really had run out of quarters. "Ralph, I'm at a pay phone with no more money, so let's be brief: I just heard about Durham."

"Did you feed the Sommers file to him?" he asked, voice heavy with suspicion.

"So that he could denounce me as an Ajax stooge and have every reporter in the city hounding me? Thank you, no. My client's aunt reacted with indignation to my asking her about the previous death certificate and the check; my client fired me. I'm guessing he went to Durham, but I don't know that definitely. When I find out, I'll call you. Anything else? Rossy on your butt over this?"

"The whole sixty-third floor. Although Rossy is saying it shows he was right not to trust you."

"He's just flailing in fury, looking for a target. These are the snows of summer, they won't stick on Ajax, although they may freeze me some. I'm going to see Sommers to find out what he told Durham. What about your historian, Amy Blount, the young woman who wrote up the book on Ajax? Yesterday Rossy was saying he didn't trust her not to give Ajax data to Durham. Did he ask her that?"

"She denied showing our private papers to anyone, but how else could Durham have found out who we insured back in the 1850's? We mention Birnbaum in our history, bragging that they go back with us to 1852, but not the detail Durham has, about insuring plow shipments they made to slaveholders. Now the Birnbaum lawyers are threatening us with breach of fiduciary responsibility, although whether it extends back that far—"

"Do you have Blount's phone number? I could try asking her."

The metallic voice announced that I needed another twenty-five cents. Ralph quickly told me Blount had gotten her Ph.D. in economic history at the University of Chicago last June; I could reach her through the department. "Call me when you—" he started to add, but the phone company cut us off.

I dashed through the lobby to the cab rank, but the sight of a pair of smokers huddled along the wall made me remember Don, sitting in the Ritz bar. I hesitated, then remembered my phone charger was still in Morrell's car—I wouldn't be able to call Don from the road to explain why I'd stood him up.

I found him under a fern tree in the smoking section of the bar, with two glasses of champagne in front of him. When he saw me he put out his cigarette. I bent over to kiss his cheek.

"Don—I wish you every success. With this book and with your career." I picked up a glass to toast him. "But I can't stay to drink: there's a crisis involving the players you originally came here to interview."

When I told him about Durham's pickets outside Ajax and that I wanted to go see what they were up to, he relit his cigarette. "Did anyone ever tell you you have too much energy, Vic? It'll age Morrell before his time, trying to keep up with you. I am going to sit here with my champagne, having a happy conversation about Rhea Wiell's book with my literary agent. I will then drink your glass as well. If you learn anything as you bounce around Chicago like a pinball in the hands of a demented wizard, I will listen breathlessly to your every word."

"For which I will charge you a hundred dollars an hour." I swallowed a large gulp of champagne, then handed him the glass. I curbed my impulse to dart across the lobby to the elevators: the image of myself as a pinball careening around the city was embarrassing—although it kept recurring to me as the afternoon progressed.

XII

Pinball Wizard

I bounced first to the Ajax building on Adams. Durham only had a small band of pickets out—in the middle of a workday most people don't have time to demonstrate. Durham himself led the charge, surrounded by his cadre of Empower Youth Energy members, their eyes watching the passersby with the sullenness of men prepared to fight on a moment's notice. Behind them came a small group of ministers and community leaders from the South and West Sides, followed by the usual handful of earnest college students. They chanted "Justice now," "No high-rises on the bones of slaves," and "No reparations for slaveowners." I walked in step with one of the students, who welcomed me as a convert to the fold.

"I didn't realize Ajax had benefited so much from slavery," I said.

"It's not just that, but did you hear what happened yesterday? They sicced a detective on this poor old woman who had just lost her husband. They cashed his life-insurance check and then, like, pretended she had done it and sent this detective down to accuse her, right in the middle of the funeral."

"What?" I shouted.

"Really sucks, doesn't it. Here—you can read the details." He thrust a broadsheet at me. My name jumped out at me.

AJAX—HAVE YOU NO MERCY?
WARSHAWSKI—HAVE YOU NO SHAME?
BIRNBAUM—HAVE YOU NO COMPASSION?

Where is the widow's mite? Gertrude Sommers, a God-fearing woman, a churchgoing woman, a taxpaying woman, lost her son. Then she lost her husband. Must she lose her dignity, as well?

Ajax Insurance cashed her husband's life-insurance policy ten years ago. When he died last week, they sent their tame detective, V I Warshawski, to accuse Sister Sommers of stealing it. In the middle of the funeral, in front of her friends and loved ones, they shamed her.

Warshawski, we all have to make a living, but must you do it on the bodies of the poor? Ajax, make good the wrong. Pay the widow her mite. Repair the damage you have done to the grandchildren of slaves. Birnbaum, give back the money you made with Ajax on the backs of slaves. No Holocaust restitution until you make the African-American community whole.

I could feel the blood drumming in my head. No wonder Ralph was angry—but why should he take it out on me? It wasn't his name that was being slandered. I almost jumped out of the line to tackle Alderman Durham, but in the nick of time I imagined the scene on television—the EYE team wrestling with me as I screamed invective, the alderman shaking his head more in sorrow than anger and declaiming something sanctimonious to the camera.

I watched, fuming, as the circle of marchers brought Durham parallel to me. He was a big, broad-shouldered man in a black-and-tan houndstooth jacket which looked as though it had been made to measure, so carefully did the checks line up along the smooth-fitting seams. His face gleamed with excitement behind his muttonchop whiskers.

Since I couldn't punch him, I folded the broadsheet into my purse and ran down Adams toward my car. A cab would have been faster, but my rage needed a physical outlet. By the time I reached Canal Street, the soles of my feet throbbed from running in pumps on city pavement. I was lucky I hadn't sprained an ankle. I stood outside my car gulping in air, my throat dry.

As my pulse returned to normal, I wondered where Bull Durham had gotten the money for custom tailoring. Was someone paying him to harass Ajax and the Birnbaums—not to mention me? Of course, all aldercreatures have plenty of chances to stick their fingers in the till in perfectly legal ways—I was so furious with him I wanted to assume the worst.

I needed a phone, and I needed water. As I looked for a convenience store where I could buy a bottle, I passed a wireless shop. I bought another in-car charger: my life would be easier this afternoon if I was plugged in.

Before I got onto the expressway to track down my client—ex-client—I called Mary Louise on my private office line. She was understandably upset at my leaving her holding the bag. I explained how that had happened, then read her Bull Durham's broadsheet.

"Good grief, he's got a nerve! What do you want to do about it?"

"Start with a statement. Something like this:

"In his zeal to make political hay out of Gertrude Sommers's loss, Alderman Durham overlooked a few things, including the facts. When Gertrude Sommers's husband died last week, the Delaney Funeral Parlor humiliated her by halting the funeral just as she took her seat in the chapel. They did so because her husband's life-insurance policy had been cashed some years ago. The family briefly employed investigator V I Warshawski to get at the facts of what happened. Contrary to Alderman Durham's claims, Ajax Insurance did not hire Warshawski. Warshawski was not at Aaron Sommers's funeral and did not see or meet the unfortunate widow until the following week. It is inconceivable that Warshawski would ever interrupt a funeral in the fashion the alderman is claiming. If Alderman Durham was utterly mistaken about the facts of Warshawski's involvement in the case, are his other statements open to the same questions?"

Mary Louise read it back to me. We tweaked it a few times, then she agreed to phone or e-mail it to the reporters who had been calling. If Beth Blacksin or Murray wanted to talk to me in person, she should tell them to come to my office around six-thirty—although if they were like the rest of the Chicago media, they would probably be camped outside the doors of members of the Birnbaum family, hoping to accost them.

A cop tapped my parking meter and made an ugly comment. I put the car in gear and started down Madison toward the expressway.

"Do you know what the Birnbaum part of Durham's handout is about?" Mary Louise asked.

"Apparently Ajax insured the Birnbaums back in the 1850's. Part of the vast Birnbaum holdings came from something in the South. Ajax execs are steaming over how Durham got that information."

As I oozed onto the expressway I was glad I'd bought the water: traffic seems to run freely these days only between ten at night and six the next morning. At two-thirty, the trucks heading south on the Ryan formed a solid wall. I put Mary Louise on hold while I slid my Mustang in between an eighteen-wheel UPS truck and a long flatbed with what looked like a reactor coil strapped to it.

Before hanging up, I asked her to dig up Amy Blount's home phone number and address. "Phone them to me here in my car, but don't call her yourself. I don't know yet if I want to talk to her."

The flatbed behind me gave a loud hoot that made me jump: I had let three car lengths open up in front of me. I scooted forward.

Mary Louise said, "Before you go, I tracked down those men Aaron Sommers worked with at South Branch Scrap Metal. The ones who bought life insurance from Rick Hoffman along with Mr. Sommers."

The Durham attack on me personally had driven the earlier business from my mind. I'd forgotten to tell Mary Louise the client had fired me, so she'd gone ahead with the investigation and had found three of the four men still alive. Claiming to be doing an independent quality check for the company, she'd persuaded the policyholders to call the Midway Agency. The men said their policies were still intact; she'd double-checked with the carrier. The third man had died eight years ago. His funeral had been duly paid for by Ajax. So whatever fraud had been committed, it wasn't some wholesale looting by Midway or Hoffman of those particular burial policies. Not that it really mattered at this point, but I thanked her for the extra effort—she'd done a lot in a short morning—and turned my attention to the traffic.

When I reached the Stevenson cutoff, my motion slowed to something more like a turtle on Valium than a pinball—construction, now in its third year, cut off half the lanes. The Stevenson Expressway is the key to the industrial zone along the city's southwest corridor. Truck traffic along it is always heavy; with the construction and the afternoon rush building, we all bumped along at about ten miles an hour.

At Kedzie I was glad to leave the expressway for the maze of plants and scrap yards alongside it. Even though the day was clear, down here among the factories the air turned blue-grey from smoke. I passed yards full of rusting cars, yards making outboard motors, a rebar mill, and a mountain of yellowish salt, ominous portent of the winter ahead. The roads were deeply rutted. I drove cautiously, my car slung too low to the ground for the axle to survive a major hole. Trucks jumped past me with a happy disregard of any traffic signs.

Even with a good detail map I blundered a few times. It was a quarter past three, fifteen minutes after Isaiah Sommers's shift ended, before I jolted into the yard of the Docherty Engineering Works. A roughly graveled area, it was as scarred by heavy trucks as the surrounding streets. A fourteen-wheeler was snorting at a loading dock when I got out of the Mustang.

It was my lucky afternoon—it looked as though the seven-to-three shift was just leaving the shop. I leaned against my car, watching men straggle through a side door. Isaiah Sommers appeared about halfway through the exodus. He was talking to a couple of other men, laughing in an easy way that took me by surprise: when I'd met him he'd been hunched and surly. I waited until he'd clapped his coworkers on the shoulder and gone on to his own truck before straightening up to follow him.

"Mr. Sommers?"

The smile vanished, leaving his face in the guarded lines I'd seen the other night. "Oh. It's you. What do you want?"

I pulled the broadsheet from my purse and handed it to him. "I see the steps you took on your own led you straight to Alderman Durham. There are a few factual errors, but it's having quite a galvanizing effect on the city: you should be pleased."

He read the sheet with the same slow concentration he'd given my contract. "Well?"

"You know as well as I that I wasn't present at your uncle's funeral. Did you tell Mr. Durham that I was?"

"Maybe he put the two pieces of the story together wrong, but, yes, I did talk to him. Told him about you accusing my aunt." He stuck his jaw out pugnaciously.

"I'm not here to play he-said, she-said with you but to find out why you went out of your way to pillory me in this public way, instead of trying to work things out in private."

"My aunt—she doesn't have money or connections or a way to get even when someone like you comes along to accuse her unjustly."

Several men passed us, looking us over curiously. One of them called a greeting to Sommers. He flipped up a palm, but kept his angry gaze on me.

"Your aunt feels bereft. She needs someone to blame, so she's blaming me. Almost ten years ago, someone using your aunt's name cashed a check for the policy, with a death certificate claiming your uncle was dead to back up the claim. Either your aunt did it, or someone else. But her name was on the check. I had to ask her. You've fired me, so I won't be asking any more questions, but don't you wonder how it got there?"

"The company did it. The company did it and hired you to frame me, like it says here." He pointed at the broadsheet, but his voice lacked conviction.

"It's a possibility," I conceded. "It's a possibility the company did it. We'll never know, of course."

"Why not?"

I smiled. "I have no reason to look into it. You could hire someone else to do so, but it would cost you a fortune. Of course it's much easier to toss accusations around than it is to look for facts. It's the American way these days, isn't it: find a scapegoat instead of a fact."

His face was bunched in confusion. I took the broadsheet from him and turned back to my car. The phone, which I'd left attached to the charger, was ringing—Mary Louise, with Amy Blount's details. I scribbled them down and started the car.

"Wait," Isaiah Sommers yelled.

He shook off someone who'd stopped to talk to him and ran over to my car. I put it in park and looked up at him, my brows raised, my expression bland.

He fumbled for words, then blurted out, "What do you think?"

"About—"

"You said it's a possibility that the company cashed in the policy. Is that what you think?"

I turned off the engine. "To be honest, no. I won't say it's impossible: I uncovered claims fraud at that company once before, but it was under a different management team, which had to resign when the news got out. The thing is, it would mean collusion between someone in the company and the agent, since the agency deposited the check, but the claims manager made no demur about bringing the file up where I could see it." It's true Rossy had put me through a song and dance to keep me from examining the complete file—but Edelweiss had only been involved with Ajax for four months, so I didn't see how he could possibly be part of an Ajax life-insurance fraud.

"The agent is a more likely candidate. Although none of the other policies Hoffman sold at your uncle's workplace was fraudulently cashed, the check was paid through Midway. It's also possible your uncle did it, for reasons you might never know or you might find very painful to know. Or some other family member. And before you blow your stack and get on to Bull Durham from the nearest phone, I don't seriously think it was your aunt, not after talking to her. But your family or the agency would be the two places I would look. If I was looking."

He slammed the roof of my car in frustration. He was strong enough that the car bounced slightly.

"Look here, Ms. Warashki. I don't know who to believe, or who to listen to. My wife—she thought I should go talk to Alderman Durham. Camilla Rawlings, the lady who gave me your name to begin with, she already chewed me out for firing you: she thinks I should make my peace with you. But what can I believe? Mr. Durham, he said he had proof the insurance company profited from slavery, and this is one more cover-up, and no offense, but you being white, how can you understand?"

I got out of the car so he wouldn't have to bend over and I wouldn't get a crick in my neck looking up. "Mr. Sommers, I can't ever, completely, but I do try to listen empathically—and impartially—to whatever I hear. The situation with your aunt, I realize it's complicated by America's history. If I want to ask her how her name got to be on that check, then you and your wife and your aunt see me as a white woman, someone in league with the company to defraud you. But if I start screaming in chorus with you—company cover-up! fraud!—when I have no facts, then I'm useless as a detective. My only lodestar is sticking to the truth—as far as I can know it. It's a costly decision—I lose clients like you, I lost a wonderful man in Camilla's brother. I'm not always right, but I have to stick to the truth or be buffeted like a leaf by every wind that blows."

It took me a long time to get over my breakup with Conrad Rawlings. I love Morrell, he's a great guy—but Conrad and I were attuned in a way that you only find once in a very blue moon.

Sommers's face contorted with strain. "Would you consider going back to work for me?"

"I'd consider it. I'd be a little wary, though."

He nodded in a kind of rueful understanding, then blurted out, "I'm sorry about Durham getting the facts mixed up. I do have cousins, one anyway, that could have gone and done it. But you see, it's painful, too painful, to expose my family like that. And if it was my cousin Colby, then, hell, I'll never see the money again. I'd be out the price of the funeral and the price of your fee, besides making my family ashamed in public."

"It's a serious problem. I can't advise you on it."

He shut his eyes tightly for a moment. "Is there—do you still owe me any more time from my five hundred dollars?"

He'd had an hour and a half coming to him before Mary Louise checked with the men at South Branch Scrap Metal. Any more work would be with the meter running again.

"About an hour," I said gruffly, cursing myself.

"Could you—is there anything you could find out about the agent in just an hour?"

"You going to call Mr. Durham and tell him he made a mistake? I have a press interview scheduled at six-thirty; I don't want to mention your name if I'm working for you."

He took a breath. "I'll call him. If you'll ask a few questions of the insurance agency."

XIII

Secret Agent

Family spokesman Andy Birnbaum, great-grandson of the patriarch who parlayed a scrap-metal pushcart into one of America's great fortunes, said the family is bewildered by Durham's accusations. The Birnbaum Foundation has supported inner-city education, arts, and economic development for four decades. Birnbaum added that relations of the African-American community with both the Birnbaum Corporation and its foundation have been mutually supportive, and he is sure that if Alderman Durham sits down to talk, the alderman will realize there has been a misunderstanding."

I got that sound bite on the radio as I was riding back into the city. The inbound traffic was heavy but moving fast, so I didn't pay close attention until my own name jumped out at me.

"Investigator V I Warshawski said in a written statement that Durham's accusations that she had interrupted Aaron Sommers's funeral with demands for money are a complete fabrication. Joseph Posner, who is lobbying hard for Illinois to pass the Holocaust Asset Recovery Act, said that Durham's charges against Ajax were a red herring to keep the legislature from considering the act. He said Durham's anti-Semitic comments were a disgrace to the memory of the dead, but that as the Sabbath started in a few hours he would not violate its peace by appearing in public to confront the alderman."

Thank heavens we were at least spared Joseph Posner joining the fray just now. I couldn't absorb any more news; I turned to music. One of the classical stations was soothing the commuter's savage breast with something very modern and spiky. The other was running a high-voltage ad for Internet access. I turned off the radio altogether and followed the lake south, back to Hyde Park.

Given Howard Fepple's lackadaisical attitude toward his business, there was only an outside chance that I'd find him still in his office at four-thirty on Friday. Still, when you're a pinball, you bounce off all the levers in the hopes of landing in the money. And this time I had a bit of luck—or whatever you'd call the chance to talk to Fepple again. He was not only in but he'd installed fresh lightbulbs, so that the torn linoleum, the grime, and his eager expression when I opened the door all showed up clearly.

"Mr. Fepple," I said heartily. "Glad to see you haven't given up on the business yet."

He turned away from me, his eager look replaced by a scowl. It obviously wasn't the hope of seeing me that had led him to put on a suit and tie.

"You know, an amazing thought occurred to me when I was driving back from seeing Isaiah Sommers this afternoon. Bull Durham knew about me. He knew about the Birnbaums. He knew about Ajax. But even though he went on for days about the injustice to the Sommers family, he didn't seem to know about you."

"You don't have an appointment," he muttered, still not looking at me. "You can leave now."

"Walk-in business," I chirped brightly. "You need to cultivate it. So let's talk about that policy you sold Aaron Sommers."

"I told you, it wasn't me, it was Rick Hoffman."

"Same difference. Your agency. Your legal liability for any wrongdoing. My client isn't interested in dragging this out in court for years, although he could sue you for a bundle under ERISA—you had a fiduciary responsibility to his uncle, which you violated. He'd be happy if you'd cut him a check for the ten thousand that the policy was worth."

"He's not your—" he blurted, then stopped.

"My, my, Howard. Who has been talking to you? Was it Mr. Sommers himself? No, that can't be right, or you'd know he'd brought me back in to finish the investigation. So it must have been Alderman Durham. If that's the case, you are going to have so much publicity you'll be turning business away. I have an interview with Channel Thirteen in a little bit, and they will be salivating when they hear that your agency has been tipping off Bull Durham about your own customers' affairs."

"You're all wet," he said, curling his lip. "I couldn't talk to Durham—he's made it clear he doesn't have any use for whites."

"Now I'm really curious." I settled myself in the rickety chair in front of his desk. "I'm dying to see who you're all dolled up for."

"I have a date. I do have a social life that has nothing to do with insurance. I want you to leave so I can close up my office."

"In a little bit. As soon as you answer some questions. I want to see the file on Aaron Sommers."

His carpet of freckles turned a deeper orange. "You have a helluva nerve. Those are private papers, none of your damned business."

"They are my client's business. One way or another, either by you cooperating now or by my getting a court order, you're going to show me the file. So let's do it now."

"Go get your court order if you can. My father trusted me with his business; I am not going to let him down."

It was a strange and rather sad attempt at bravado. "Okay. I'll get a court order. One other thing. Rick Hoffman's notebook. That little black book he carried around with him, ticking off his clients' payments. I want to see it."

"Join the crowd," he snapped. "Everyone in Chicago wants to see his notebook, but I don't have it. He took it home with him every night like it was the secret of the atom bomb. And when he died it was at his home. If I knew where his son was, maybe I'd know where the damned notebook was. But that creep is probably in an insane asylum someplace. He's not in Chicago, at any rate."

His phone rang. He jumped on it so fast it might have been a hundred-dollar bill on the sidewalk.

"There's someone with me right now," he blurted into the mouthpiece. "Right, the woman detective." He listened for a minute, said, "Okay, okay," jotted what looked like numbers on a scrap of paper, and hung up.

He turned off his desk lamp and made a big show of locking his filing cabinets. When he came around to open the door, I had no choice but to get up, as well. We rode the elevator down to the lobby, where he surprised me by going up to the guard.

"See this lady, Collins? She's been coming around my office, making threats. Can you make sure she doesn't get into the building again tonight?"

The guard looked me up and down before saying, "Sure thing,

Mr. Fepple," without much enthusiasm. Fepple went outside with me. When I congratulated him on a successful tactic, he smirked before striding off down the street. I watched him go into the pizza restaurant on the corner. They had a phone in the entryway, which he stopped to use.

I joined a couple of drunks outside a convenience store across the street. They were arguing about a man named Clive and what Clive's sister had said about one of them, but they broke off to try to cadge the price of a bottle from me. I moved away from them, still watching Fepple.

After about five minutes he came out, looked around cautiously, saw me, and darted toward a shopping center on the north side of the street. I started after him, but one of the drunks grabbed me, telling me not to be such a stuck-up bitch. I stuck a knee in his stomach and jerked my arm free. While he shouted obscenities I ran north, but I was still in my pumps. This time the left heel gave and I tumbled to the concrete. By the time I got myself collected, Fepple had disappeared.

I cursed myself, Fepple, and the drunks with equal ferocity. By a miracle, damage was limited to the shreds in my panty hose and a bloody scrape on my left leg and thigh. In the fading daylight I couldn't tell if I'd ruined my skirt, a silky black number that I was rather fond of. I limped back to my car, where I used part of my bottle of water to clean the blood from my leg. The skirt had some dirt ground into it, fraying the fabric surface. I picked at the gravel bits disconsolately. Maybe when it was cleaned the torn threads wouldn't show.

Leaning back in the front seat with my eyes shut, I wondered whether it was worthwhile trying to get back into the Hyde Park Bank building. Even if I could charm my way past the guard in my current disarray, if I took anything, Fepple would know it had been me. That project could wait until Monday.

I still had over an hour before I was due to meet Beth Blacksin— I should just go home and clean up properly for my interview. On the other hand, Amy Blount, Ph.D., the young woman who'd written Ajax's history, lived only three blocks from the bank. I called the number Mary Louise had dug up for me.

Ms. Blount was home. In her polite, aloof way she acknowledged that we'd met. When I explained that I wanted to ask some questions about Ajax, she turned from aloof to frosty.

"Mr. Rossy's secretary has already asked me those questions. I find them offensive. I won't answer them from you any more than from him."

"Sorry, Ms. Blount, I wasn't very clear. Ajax didn't send me to you. I don't know what questions Rossy wants to ask you, but they're probably different from mine. Mine come from a client who's trying to find out what happened to a life-insurance policy. I don't think you know the answer, but I'd like to talk to you because—" Because of what? Because I was so frustrated at being stiffed by Fepple, defamed by Durham, that I was clutching at any straw? "Because I cannot figure out what's going on and I'd like to talk to someone who understands Ajax. I'm in the neighborhood; I could stop by now for ten minutes if you can spare the time."

After a pause, she said coldly she would hear what I had to say but couldn't promise she'd answer any questions.

She lived in a shabby courtyard building on Cornell, the kind of haphazardly maintained property that students can afford. Even so, as I knew from the plaint of an old friend whose son was starting medical school down here, Blount probably paid six or seven hundred a month for the broken glass on the sidewalk, her badly hung lobby door, and the hole in the stairwell wall.

Blount stood in the open door to her studio apartment, watching while I climbed the third flight of stairs. Here at home, her dreadlocks hung loosely about her face. Instead of the prim tweed suit she'd worn to Ajax, she had on jeans and a big shirt. She ushered me in politely but without cordiality, waving a hand at a hardwood chair while seating herself in the swivel desk chair at her work station.

Except for a futon with a bright kente cover and a print of a woman squatting behind a basket, the room was furnished with monastic severity. It was lined on all sides by white pasteboard bookshelves. Even the tiny eating alcove had shelves fitted around a clock.

"Ralph Devereux told me you had a degree in economic history. Is that how you came to be involved with writing the Ajax history?"

She nodded without speaking.

"What did you do your dissertation on?"

"Is this relevant to your client's story, Ms. Warshawski?"

I raised my brows. "Polite conversation, Ms. Blount. But that's right, you said you wouldn't answer any questions. You said you had already heard from Bertrand Rossy, so you know that Alderman Durham has had Ajax under—"

"His secretary," she corrected me. "Mr. Rossy is too important to call me himself."

Her voice was so toneless that I couldn't be sure whether her intent was ironic. "Still, he made the questions take place. So you know Durham's picketing the Ajax building, claiming that Ajax and the Birnbaums owe restitution to the African-American community for the money they both made from slavery. I suppose Rossy accused you of supplying Durham the information out of the Ajax archives."

She nodded fractionally, her eyes wary.

"The other piece of Durham's protest concerns me personally. Have you encountered the Midway Insurance Agency over in the bank building? Howard Fepple is the rather ineffectual present owner, but thirty years ago one of his father's agents sold a policy to a man named Sommers." I outlined the Sommers family problem. "Now Durham has hold of the story. Based on your work at Ajax, I'm wondering if you have any ideas on who might give the alderman such detailed inside information about both the company history and this current claim. Sommers complained to the alderman, but the Durham protest had one detail that I don't think Sommers would have known: the fact that Ajax insured the Birnbaum Corporation in the years before the Civil War. I'm assuming that information is accurate, or Rossy wouldn't have called you. Had his secretary call you."

When I paused, Blount said, "It is, sort of. That is, the original Birnbaum, the one who started the family fortune, was insured by Ajax in the 1850's."

"What do you mean, sort of?" I asked.

"In 1858, Mordecai Birnbaum lost a load of steel plows he was sending to Mississippi when the steamship blew up on the Illinois River. Ajax paid for it. I suppose that's what Alderman Durham is referring to." She spoke in a rapid monotone. I hoped when she lectured to students she had more animation, or they'd all be asleep.

"Steel plows?" I repeated, my attention diverted. "They existed before the Civil War?"

She smiled primly. "John Deere invented the steel plow in 1830. In 1847 he set up his first major plant and retail store here in Illinois."

"So the Birnbaums were already an economic power in 1858."

"I don't think so. I think it was the Civil War that made the family fortune, but the Ajax archives didn't include a lot of specifics—I was guessing from the list of assets being insured. The Birnbaum plows were only a small part of the ship's cargo."

"In your opinion, who could have told Durham about Birnbaum's plow shipment?"

"Is this a subtle way to get me to confess?"

She could have asked the question in a humorous vein—but she didn't. I made an effort not to lose my own temper in return. "I'm open to all possibilities, but I have to consider the available facts. You had access to the archives. Perhaps you shared the data with Durham. But if you didn't, perhaps you have some ideas on who did."

"So you did come here to accuse me." She set her jaw in an uncompromising line.

I sank my face into my hands, suddenly tired of the matter. "I came here hoping to get better information than I have. But let it be. I have an interview with Channel Thirteen to discuss the whole sorry business; I need to go home to change."

She tightened her lips. "Do you plan to accuse me on air?"

"I actually didn't come here to accuse you of anything at all, but you're so suspicious of me and my motives that I can't imagine you'd believe any assurances I gave you. I came here hoping that a trained observer like you would have seen something that would give me a new way to think about what's going on."

She looked at me uncertainly. "If I told you I didn't give Durham the files, would you believe me?"

I spread my hands. "Try me."

She took a breath, then spoke rapidly, looking at the books over her computer. "I happen not to support Mr. Durham's ideas. I am fully cognizant of the racial injustices that still exist in this country. I have researched and written about black economic and commercial history, so I am more familiar with the history of these injustices than most: they run deep, and they run wide. I took the job of writing that Ajax history, for instance, because I'm having a hard time getting academic history or economics programs to pay attention to me, outside of African-American studies, which are too often marginalized for me to find interesting. I need to earn something while I'm job-hunting. Also, the Ajax archives will make an interesting monograph. But I don't believe in focusing on African-Americans as victims: it makes us seem pitiable to white America, and as long as we are pitiable we will not be respected." She flushed, as if embarrassed to reveal her beliefs to a stranger.

I thought of Lotty's angry vehemence with Max on the subject of Jews as victims. I nodded slowly and told Blount that I could believe her.

"Besides," she added, her color still deepened, "it would seem immoral to me to make the Ajax files available to an outsider, when they had trusted me with their private documents."

"Since you didn't feed inside Ajax information to the alderman, can you think who might have?"

She shook her head. "It's such a big company. And the files aren't exactly secret, at least they weren't when I was doing my research. They keep all of the old material in their company library, in boxes. Hundreds of boxes, as a matter of fact. Recent material they guarded carefully, but the first hundred years—it was more a question of having the patience to wade through it than any particular difficulty gaining access to it. Although you do have to ask the librarian to see it—still, anyone who wanted to study those papers could probably get around that difficulty."

"So it might be an employee, someone with a grudge, or someone who could be bribed? Or perhaps a zealous member of Alderman Durham's organization?"

"Any or all of those could be reasonable possibilities, but I have no names to put forward. Still, thirty-seven hundred people of color hold low-level clerical or manual-laboring positions in the company. They are underpaid, underrepresented in supervisory positions, and often are treated to overt racial slurs. Any of them could become angry enough to undertake an act of passive sabotage."

I stood up, wondering if someone in the Sommers extended family was among the low-level clerks at Ajax. I thanked Amy Blount for being willing to talk to me and left her one of my cards, in case anything else occurred to her. As she walked me to the door I stopped to admire the picture of the squatting woman. Her head was bent over the basket in front of her; you didn't see her face.

"It's by Lois Mailou Jones," Ms. Blount said. "She also refused to be a victim."

XIV

Running the Tape

Late that night, I lay in the dark next to Morrell, fretting uselessly, endlessly, about the day. My mind bounced—like a pinball—from Rhea Wiell to Alderman Durham, my fury with him rising each time I thought of that flyer he was handing out in the Ajax plaza. When I tried to put that to rest I'd go back to Amy Blount, to Howard Fepple, and finally to my gnawing worries about Lotty.

When I'd gone to my office from Amy Blount's place, I'd found the copies of the Paul Radbuka video the Unblinking Eye had made for me, along with the stills of Radbuka.

My long afternoon dealing with Sommers and Fepple had pushed Radbuka out of my mind. At first I only stared at the packet, trying to remember what I'd wanted from the Eye. When I saw the stills of Radbuka's face, I recalled my promise to Lotty to get her a copy of the video today. Numb with fatigue, I was thinking I might hang on to it until I saw her on Sunday at Max's, when she phoned.

"Victoria, I'm trying to be civilized, but have you not had my messages this afternoon?"

I explained that I hadn't had a chance to check with my answering service. "In about fifteen minutes I'm talking to a reporter about the charges that Bull Durham's been flinging at me, so I was trying to organize my response into sincere, succinct nuggets."

"Bull Durham? The man who's been protesting the Holocaust

Asset Recovery Act? Don't tell me he's involved now with Paul Radbuka!"

I blinked. "No. He's involved in a case I've been working on. Insurance fraud involving a South Side family."

"And that takes precedence over responding to messages from me?"

"Lotty!" I was outraged. "Alderman Durham handed out flyers today defaming me. He marched around a public space bellowing insults about me through a bullhorn. It doesn't seem extraordinary that I had to respond to that. I walked into my office five minutes ago. I haven't even seen my messages."

"Yes, I see," she said. "I—but I need some support, too. I want to see this man's video, Victoria. I want to know that you're trying to help me. That you won't aban—that you won't forget our—"

Her voice was panicky; she was flailing about for words in a way that made my insides twist. "Lotty, please, how could I forget our friendship? Or ever abandon you? As soon as I finish with this interview, I'll be right over. Say in an hour?"

When we hung up I checked my messages. She'd phoned three times. Beth Blacksin had phoned once, to say she'd love to talk to me but could I come to the Global building, since she was jammed up with editing all the interviews and demonstrations of the day. She'd seen Murray Ryerson—he'd join us at the studio. I thought wistfully of my cot in the back room but gathered up my things and drove back downtown.

Beth spent twenty minutes taping me while she and Murray peppered me with questions. I was being careful not to implicate my client, but I freely tossed them Howard Fepple's name—it was time someone besides me started pushing on him. Beth was gleeful enough to get this exclusive new source that she happily shared what she had with me, but neither she nor Murray had any idea who had given Durham the information on the Birnbaums.

"I got thirty seconds with the alderman, who says it's common knowledge," Murray said. "I talked to the Birnbaum legal counsel, who said it's overblown ancient history. I couldn't get to the woman who wrote their history, Amy Blount—someone at Ajax suggested it was her."

"I talked to her," I said smugly. "I'd bet hard against her. It has to be another Ajax insider. Or maybe someone in the Birnbaum company with a grudge. You talk to Bertrand Rossy? I gather he's fulminating—the Swiss probably aren't used to street demonstrations. If Durham hadn't libeled me, I'd be chortling over it."

"You know that piece we did on Wednesday on Paul Radbuka?" Beth said, changing the subject to something she cared about personally. "We've had about a hundred and thirty e-mails from people who say they know his little friend Miriam. My assistant's tracking them down. Most of them are unstable glory-seekers, but it will be such a coup if one of them turns out to be the real deal. Just think if we reunite them on-air!"

"I hope you're not building that up on-air," I said sharply. "It may turn out to be just that: air."

"What?" Beth stared at me. "You think he made up his friend? No, Vic, you're wrong about that."

Murray, whose six-eight frame had been curled against a filing cabinet, suddenly stood up straight and began pelting me with questions: what inside dope did I have on Paul Radbuka? What did I know about his playmate Miriam? What did I know about Rhea Wiell?

"Nothing on all of the above," I said. "I haven't talked to the guy. But I met Rhea Wiell this morning."

"She's not a fraud, Vic," Beth said sharply.

"I know she's not. She's not a fraud and she's not a con artist. But she believes in herself so intensely that—I don't know, I can't explain it," I finished helplessly, struggling to articulate why her look of ecstasy when she discussed Paul Radbuka had unnerved me so much. "I agree—it doesn't seem possible that someone as experienced as Wiell could be conned. But—well, I guess I won't have an opinion until I meet Radbuka," I finished lamely.

"When you do, you'll really believe in him," Beth promised.

She left a minute later to edit my remarks for the ten o'clock news. Murray tried to talk me into a drink. "You know, Warshawski, we work together so well, it'd be a shame not to get back in the habit."

"Oh, Murray, you sweet-talker, you, I can see how badly you need your own private angle on this stuff. I can't stay tonight—it's vital that I get to Lotty Herschel's place in the next half hour."

He followed me down the hall to the security station while I handed in my pass. "What's the real story for you here, Warshawski? Radbuka and Wiell? Or Durham and the Sommers family?"

I frowned up at him. "They both are. That's the problem. I can't quite focus on either of them."

"Durham is about the slickest politico in town these days next to the mayor. Be careful how you tangle with him. Say hey to the doc for me, okay?" He squeezed my shoulder affectionately and turned back up the hall.

I've known Lotty Herschel since I was an undergraduate at the University of Chicago. I was a blue-collar girl on an upscale campus, feeling rawly out of place, when I met her—she was providing medical advice to an abortion underground where I volunteered. She took me under her wing, giving me the kind of social skills I'd lost when I lost my mother, keeping me from losing my way in those days of drugs and violent protest, taking time from a dense-packed schedule to cheer my successes and condole over failures. She'd even gone to some college basketball games to see me play—true friendship, since sports of all kind bore her. But it was my athletic scholarship that made my education possible, so she supported my doing my best at it. If she was collapsing now, if something terrible was wrong with her—I couldn't even finish the thought, it was so frightening to me.

She'd recently moved to a high-rise on the lakefront, to one of the beautiful old buildings where you can watch the sun rise with nothing between you and water but Lake Shore Drive and a strip of park. She used to live in a two-flat a short walk from her storefront clinic, but her one concession to aging was to give up on being a landlady in a neighborhood full of drug-dealing housebreakers. Max and I had both been relieved to see her in a building with an indoor garage.

When I left my car with her doorman, it was only eight o'clock. The day seemed to have been spinning on so long I was sure we must have come round the other side of dark to begin a new one.

Lotty was waiting in the hall for me when I got off the elevator, making a valiant effort at composure. Even though I held the envelope of stills and video out to her, she didn't snatch it from me but invited me in to her living room, offering me a drink. When I said I only wanted water, she still ignored the envelope, trying to make a joke that I must be ill if I wanted water instead of whisky. I smiled, but the deep circles under her dark eyes disturbed me. I didn't comment on her appearance, just asking as she turned to go to the kitchen if she would bring me a piece of fruit or cheese.

She seemed to really look at me for the first time. "You haven't eaten? I can see from the lines on your face that you're exhausted. Stay in here; I'll fix you something."

This was more like her usual brisk manner. I was slightly reassured, slumping against her couch and dozing until she returned with a tray. Cold chicken, carrot sticks, a small salad, and slices of the thick bread a Ukrainian nurse at the hospital bakes for her. I tried not to spring on the food as if I were one of my own dogs.

While I ate, Lotty watched me, as if keeping her eyes from the envelope by an act of will. She kept up a flow of random chatter—had I decided to go away with Morrell for the weekend, would we make it back for Sunday afternoon's concert, Max was expecting forty or fifty people at his house for dinner afterward, but he—and especially Calia—would miss me if I didn't come.

I finally interrupted the flow. "Lotty, are you afraid to look at the pictures because of what you will see or because of what you may not see?"

She gave the ghost of a smile. "Acute of you, my dear. A little of both, I think. But—if you will run the tape for me, maybe I am ready to see it. Max warned me that the man was not prepossessing."

We went to the back bedroom she uses for television and loaded the tape into the VCR. I glanced at Lotty, but the fear in her face was so acute that I couldn't bear to watch her. As Paul Radbuka recounted his nightmares and his heartbreaking cries for his childhood friend, I kept my eyes glued to him. When we'd seen everything, including the "Exploring Chicago" segment with Rhea Wiell and Arnold Praeger, Lotty asked in a thread of a voice to return to Radbuka's interview.

I ran it through for her twice more, but when she wanted a third rerun I refused: her face was grey with strain. "You're torturing yourself with this, Lotty. Why?"

"I—the whole thing is hard." Even though I was sitting on the floor next to her armchair I could barely make out her words. "Something is familiar to me in what he's saying. Only I can't think, because—I can't think. I hate this. I hate seeing things that make my mind stop working. Do you believe his story?"

I made a helpless gesture. "I can't fathom it, but it's so remote from how I want to see life that my mind is rejecting it. I met the therapist yesterday—no, it was today, it just seems like a long time ago. She's a legitimate clinician, I think, but, well, fanatical. A zealot for her work in general and most particularly for this guy. I told her I wanted to interview Radbuka, to see if he could be related to these people you and Max know, but she's protecting him. He's not in the phone book, either as Paul Radbuka or Paul Ulrich, so I'm sending Mary Louise out to all the Ulrichs in Chicago. Maybe he's still living in his father's house, or maybe a neighbor will recognize his picture—we don't know his father's first name."

"How old would you say he is?" she asked unexpectedly.

"You mean, could he be the right age for the experiences he's claiming? You'd be a better judge of that than I, but again, it would be easier to answer if we saw him in person."

I took the stills out of the envelope, holding the three different shots so that the light shone full on them. Lotty looked at them a long time but finally shook her head helplessly.

"Why did I imagine something definite would jump out at me? It's what Max said to me. Resemblance is so often a trick of the expression, after all, and these are only photographs, photographs of a picture, really. I would have to see the man, and even then—after all, I'd be trying to match an adult face against a child's memory of someone who was much younger than this man is now."

I took her hand in both of mine. "Lotty, what is it you're afraid of? This is so painful for you it's breaking my heart. Is it—could he be part of your family? Do you think he's related to your mother?"

"If you knew anything of those matters, you would know better than to ask such a question," she said with a flash of her more imperious manner.

"But you do know the Radbuka family, don't you?"

She laid the pictures on the coffee table as if she were dealing cards and then proceeded to rearrange them, but she wasn't really looking at them. "I knew some members of the family many years ago. The circumstances—when I last saw them it was extremely painful. The way we parted, I mean, or anyway the whole situation. If this man is—I don't see how he could be what he says. But if he is, then I owe it to the family to try to befriend him."

"Do you want me to do some digging? Assuming I can get hold of any information to dig with?"

Her vivid, dark face was contorted with strain. "Oh, Victoria, I don't know what I want. I want the past never to have happened, or since it did and I can't change it, I want it to stay where it is, past, dead, gone. This man, I don't want to know him. But I see I will have to talk to him. Do I want you to investigate him? No, I don't want you near him. But find him for me, find him so I can talk to him, and you, you—what you can do is try to see what piece of paper convinced him his name was really Paul Radbuka."

Late that night, her unhappy, contradictory words kept tumbling through my mind. Sometime after two, I finally fell asleep, but in my dreams Bull Durham chased me until I found myself locked up with Paul Radbuka at Terezin, with Lotty on the far side of the barbed wire watching me with hurt, tormented eyes. "Keep him there among the dead," she cried.

Lotty Herschel's Story:

English Lessons

School still had three weeks to go when Hugo and I reached London, but Minna didn't think it worthwhile to register me, since my lack of English would keep me from understanding any lessons. She set me to doing chores in the house and then in the neighborhood: she would write a shopping list in her slow English script, spelling the words under her breath—incorrectly, as I saw when I learned to read and write in the new language. She would give me a pound and send me to the corner shop to buy a chop for dinner, a few potatoes, a loaf of bread. When she got home from work she would count the change twice to make sure I hadn't robbed her. Still, each week she gave me sixpence in pocket money.

Hugo, whom I saw on Sundays, was already chattering in English. I felt humiliated, the big sister not able to speak because Minna kept me barricaded behind a wall of German. She hoped day to day that I would be sent back to Vienna. "Why waste your time on English when you may leave in the morning?"

The first time she said it my heart skipped a beat. "*Mutti und Oma, die schrieben an Dich?* They wrote you? I can go home?"

"I haven't heard from Madame Butterfly," Minna spat. "In her own good time she will remember you."

Mutti had forgotten me. It hit my child's heart like a fist. A year later, when I could read English, I despised the children's books we were given in school, with their saccharine mothers and children. "My mother would never forget me. She loves me even though she is far away, and I pray every night to see her again, as I know she is praying for me and watching over me." That's what the girls in *Good Wives* or *English Orphans* would have said to Cousin Minna, boldly defiant in their trembling little-girl voices. But they didn't understand anything about life, those little girls.

Your own mother lies in bed, too worn to get up to kiss you good-bye when you get on a train, leave your city, your home, your Mutti and Oma, behind. Men in uniforms stop you, look in your suitcase, put big ugly hands on your underwear, your favorite doll, they can take these things if they want, and your mother is lying in bed, not stopping them.

Of course I knew the truth, knew that only Hugo and I could get visas and travel permits, that grown-ups weren't allowed to go to England unless someone in England gave them a job. I knew the truth, that the Nazis hated us because we were Jews, so they took away Opa's apartment with my bedroom: some strange woman was living there now with her blond child in my white-canopied bed—I had gone early one morning on foot to look at the building, with its little sign, *Juden verboten*. I knew these things, knew that my mama was hungry as we all were, but to a child, your parents are so powerful, I still half believed my parents, my Opa, would rise up and make everything go back the way it used to be.

When Minna said my mother would remember me in her own good time, she only voiced my deepest fear. I had been sent away because Mutti didn't want me. Until September, when the war started and no one could leave Austria anymore, Minna would say that at regular intervals.

Even today I'm sure she did this because she so resented my mother, Lingerl, the little butterfly with her soft gold curls, her beautiful smile, her charming manners. The only way Minna could hurt Lingerl was to hurt me. Perhaps the fact that my mother never knew made Minna twist the knife harder: she was so furious that she couldn't stab Lingerl directly that she kept on at me. Maybe that's why she was so hateful when we got the news about their fate.

The one thing I knew for sure my first summer in London, the summer of '39, was what my papa told me, that he would come if I could find him a job. Armed with a German–English dictionary, which I found in Minna's sitting room, I spent that summer walking up and down the streets near Minna's house in Kentish Town. My cheeks stained with embarrassment, I would ring doorbells and struggle to say, "Mine vater, he need job, he do all job. Garden, he make garden. House, he clean house. Coal, he bring coal, make house warm."

Eventually I ended up at the house behind Minna's. I had been watching it from my attic window because it was so different from Minna's. Hers was a narrow frame structure whose neighbors almost touched on the east and west sides. The garden was a cold oblong, as narrow as the house and only holding a few scraggly raspberry bushes. To this day I won't eat raspberries. . . .

Anyway, the house behind was made of stone, with a large garden, roses, an apple tree, a little patch of vegetables, and Claire. I knew her name because her mother and her older sister would call to her. She sat on a swing-bench under their pergola, her fair hair pulled away from her ears to hang down her back, while she pored over her books.

"Claire," her mother would call. "Teatime, darling. You'll strain your eyes reading in the sun."

Of course, I didn't understand what she was saying at first, although I could make out Claire's name, but the words were repeated every summer, so my memory blurs all those summers; in my memory I understand

Mrs. Tallmadge perfectly from the start.

Claire was studying because next year she would take her higher-school certificate; she wanted to read medicine—again, I only learned this later. The sister, Vanessa, was five years older than Claire. Vanessa had some refined little job, I don't remember what now. She was getting ready to be married that summer; that I understood clearly—all little girls understand brides and weddings, from peeping over railings at them. I would watch Vanessa come into the garden: she wanted Claire to try on a dress or a hat or admire a swatch of fabric, and finally, when she could get her sister's attention no other way, she would snatch Claire's book. Then the two would chase each other around the garden until they ended up in a laughing heap back under the pergola.

I wanted to be part of their life so desperately that at night I would lie in bed making up stories about them. Claire would be in some trouble from which I would rescue her. Claire would somehow know the details of my life with Cousin Minna and would boldly confront Minna, accuse her of all her crimes, and rescue me. I don't know why it was Claire who became my heroine, not the mother or the bride—maybe because Claire was closer to my age, so I could imagine being her. I only know that I would watch the sisters laughing together and burst into tears.

I put off their house until last because I didn't want Claire to pity me. I pictured my papa as a servant in her house; then she would never sit laughing with me on the swing. But in the letters that still passed between England and Vienna that summer, Papa kept reminding me that he needed me to get him a job. All these years later I am still bitter that Minna couldn't find a place for him at the glove factory. It's true it wasn't her factory, but she was the bookkeeper, she could talk to Herr Schatz. Every time I brought it up she screamed that she wasn't going to have people pointing a finger at her. During the war, the glove factory was working treble shifts to supply the army. . . .

Finally, one hot August morning, when I had seen Claire go into the garden with her books, I rang their doorbell. I thought if Mrs. Tallmadge answered I could manage to speak to her; if Claire was in the garden I was safe from having to face my idol. Of course it was a maid who came to the door—I should have expected that, since all of the bigger houses in our neighborhood had maids. And even the small, ugly ones like Minna's had at least a charwoman to do the heavy cleaning.

The maid said something too fast for me to understand. I only knew her tone was angry. Quickly, as she started to shut the door in my face, I blurted out in broken English that Claire wanted me.

"Claire ask, she say, you come."

The maid shut the door on me, but this time she told me to wait, a word I had learned in my weeks of doorbell ringing. By and by Claire came back with the maid.

"Oh, Susan, it's the funny little girl from over the way. I'll talk to her—you go on." When Susan disappeared, sniffing, Claire bent over and said, "I've seen you watching me over the wall, you queer little monkey. What do you want?"

I stammered out my story: father needed job. He could do anything.

"But Mother looks after the garden, and Susan cleans the house."

"Play violin. Sister—" I pantomimed Vanessa as a bride, making Claire burst into gales of laughter. "He play. Very pretty. Sister like."

Mrs. Tallmadge appeared behind her daughter, demanding to know who I was and what I wanted. She and Claire had a conversation that went on for some time, which I couldn't follow at all, except to recognize Hitler's name, and the Jews, of course. I could see that Claire was trying to persuade Mrs. Tallmadge but that the mother was obdurate—there was no money. When my English became fluent, when I got to know the family, I learned that Mr.

Tallmadge had died, leaving some money—enough to maintain the house and keep Mrs. Tallmadge and her daughters in respectable comfort—but not enough for extravagance. Sponsoring my father would have been extravagant.

At one point Claire turned to ask me about my mother. I said, Yes, she would come, too, but Claire wanted to know what kind of work my mother could perform. I stared blankly, unable to imagine such a thing. Not just because she had been sick with her pregnancy, but no one expected my mother to work. You wanted her around to make you gay, because she danced and talked and sang more beautifully than anyone. But even if my English had allowed me to express those ideas, I knew they would be a mistake.

"Sewing," I finally remembered. "Very good sewing, mother make. Makes."

"Maybe Ted?" Claire suggested.

"You can try," her mother snorted, going back into the house.

Ted was Edward Marmaduke. He was going to be Vanessa's husband. I had seen him in the garden, too, a pale Englishman with very blond hair who turned an unhealthy pinky-red under the summer sun. He would serve in Africa and Italy but come home in one piece in 1945, his face scorched to a deep brick that never really faded.

That summer of '39 he didn't want a poor immigrant couple to encumber the start of his married life with Vanessa: I heard that argument, crouched on the other side of the wall between Minna's yard and Claire's, knowing it was about me and my family but only understanding his loud "no" and from Vanessa's tone that she was trying to please both Claire and her fiancé.

Claire told me not to give up hope. "But, little monkey, you need to learn English. You have to go to school in a few weeks."

"In Vienna," I said. "I go home. I go on the school there."

Claire shook her head. "There may be war in Europe; you might not go home for a long time. No, we need to get you speaking English."

So my life changed overnight. Of course, I still lived with Minna, still ran her errands, endured her bitterness, but my heroine actually did take me to the pergola. Every afternoon she made me speak English with her. When school started, she took me to the local grammar school, introduced me to the headmistress, and helped me at odd intervals to learn my lessons.

I repaid her with lavish adoration. She was the most beautiful girl in London. She became my standard of English manners: Claire says one doesn't do that, I would say coldly to Minna. Claire says one always does this. I imitated her accent and her ways of doing things, from how she draped herself in the garden swing to how she wore her hats.

When I learned Claire was going to read medicine if she got a place at the Royal Free, that became my ambition, too.

XV

Gate Crasher

Morrell's and my brief vacation in Michigan helped drive Friday's worries to the back of my mind—thanks chiefly to Morrell's good sense. Since I was driving the outbound route I started to detour to Hyde Park, thinking I could make a quick trip in and out of Fepple's office to look for the Sommers family file. Morrell vetoed this sharply, reminding me that we'd agreed to forty-eight hours without business.

"I didn't bring my laptop, so that I wouldn't be tempted to e-mail Humane Medicine. You can stay away from an insurance agent who sounds like a disgusting specimen for that long, too, V I." Morrell took my picklocks out of my bag and stuck them in his jeans. "Anyway, I don't want to be a party to your extracurricular information-gathering techniques."

I had to laugh, despite a momentary annoyance. After all, why would I want to spoil my last few days with Morrell by bothering with a worm like Fepple? I decided not even to bother with the morning papers, which I'd stuck in my bag without reading: I didn't need to raise my blood pressure by seeing Bull Durham's attacks on me in print.

Less easy to put aside were my worries about Lotty, but our ban on business didn't include concerns about friends. I tried to describe her anguish to Morrell. He listened to me as I drove but couldn't offer much help in deciphering what lay behind her tormented speech.

"She lost her family in the war, didn't she?"

"Except for her younger brother Hugo, who went to England with her. He lives in Montreal—he runs a small chain of upscale women's boutiques in Montreal and Toronto. Her uncle Stefan, I guess he was one of her grandfather's brothers, he came to Chicago in the 1920's. And spent most of the war as a guest of the federal government in Fort Leavenworth. Forgery," I added in response to Morrell's startled question. "A master engraver who fell in love with Andrew Jackson's face but overlooked a few details. So he wasn't part of her childhood."

"She was nine or ten when she last saw her mother, then. No wonder those wartime memories are too painful for her. Didn't you say he was dead—the person named Radbuka?"

"Or she. Lotty revealed no details at all. But she did say it, said that the person no longer exists." I thought about it. "It's a peculiar construction: that person no longer exists. It could mean several things—the person died, the person changed identities, or maybe the person betrayed her in some way so that someone she loved or who she thought loved her never really existed."

"Then the pain could come from the reminder of a second loss. Don't go sleuthing after her, Vic. Let her bring the story to you when she's strong enough to."

I fixed my eyes on the road. "And if she never tells me?"

He leaned over to wipe a tear from my cheek. "It's not your failure as a friend. These are her demons, not your failures."

I didn't speak much for the rest of the ride. We were going about a hundred miles around the big U of Lake Michigan's southern end; I let the rhythm of car and road fill my mind.

Morrell had booked a room at a rambling stone inn overlooking Lake Michigan. After checking in we took a walk along the beach. It was hard to believe that this was the same lake that Chicago bordered—the long stretches of dunes, empty of everything but birds and prairie grasses, were a different world than the relentless noise and grime of the city.

Three weeks after Labor Day we had the lakefront to ourselves. Feeling the wind from the lake in my hair, making the crystalline sand along the shore sing by rubbing it with my bare heel, gave me a cocoon of peace. I felt the tension lines smooth out of my cheeks and forehead.

"Morrell—it will be very hard for me to live without you these next few months. I know this trip is exciting and that you're eager to go. I don't grudge it to you. But it will be hard—especially right now—not to have you here."

He pulled me to him. "It will be hard for me to be away from you, too, *pepaiola*. You keep me stirred up, sneezing, with your vigorous remarks."

I'd told Morrell once that my father used to call my mother and me that—one of the few Italian words he'd picked up from my mother. Pepper mill. My two *pepaiole,* he'd say, pretending to sneeze when we were haranguing him over something. You're making my nose red, okay, okay, we'll do it your way just to protect my nose. When I was a little girl he could make me burst out laughing with his fake sneezes.

"*Pepaiola,* huh—sneeze at this!" I tossed a little sand at Morrell and sprinted away from him down the beach. He chased after me, which he normally wouldn't do—he doesn't like to run, and anyway, I'm faster. I slowed so he could catch me. We spent the rest of the day avoiding all difficult topics, including his imminent departure. The air was chilly, but the lake was still warm: we swam naked in the dark, then huddled in a blanket on the beach, making love with Andromeda overhead and Orion the hunter, my talisman, rising in the east, his belt so close it seemed we might pluck it from the sky. Sunday at noon we changed reluctantly into our dress clothes and drove back into the city for the Cellini's final Chicago concert.

When we stopped for gas near the entrance to the tollway, the weekend felt officially over, so I bought the Sunday papers. Durham's protest led both the news and the op-ed sections in the *Herald-Star*. I was glad to see that my interview with Blacksin and Murray had made Durham cool his jets about me.

> Mr. Durham has dropped one of his complaints, that Chicago private investigator V I Warshawski confronted a bereaved woman in the middle of her husband's funeral. "My sources in the community were understandably devastated by the terrible inhumanity of an insurance company failing to keep its promise to pay to bury a loved one; in their agitation they may have misspoken Ms. Warshawski's role in the case."

"*May* have misspoken? Can't he come right out and say he was wrong?" I snarled at Morrell.

Murray had added a few sentences saying that my investigation was raising troubling questions about the role of both the Midway Insurance Agency and the Ajax Insurance company. Midway owner

Howard Fepple had not returned phone calls. An Ajax spokesperson said the company had uncovered a fraudulent death claim submitted ten years ago; they were trying to see how that could have occurred.

The op-ed page had an article by the president of the Illinois Insurance Institute. I read it aloud to Morrell.

Imagine that you go into Berlin, the capital of Germany, and find a large museum dedicated to the horrors of three centuries of African slavery in the United States. Then imagine that Frankfurt, Munich, Cologne, Bonn all have smaller versions of American slavery museums. That's what it's like for America to put up Holocaust museums while completely ignoring atrocities committed here against Africans and Native Americans.

Now suppose Germany passed a law saying that any American company which benefited from slavery couldn't do business in Europe. That's what Illinois wants to do with German companies. The past is a tangled country. No one's hands are clean, but if we have to stop every ten minutes to wash them before we can sell cars, or chemicals, or even insurance, commerce will grind to a halt.

"And so on. Lotty isn't alone in wanting the past to stay good and buried. Pretty slick, in a superficial kind of way."

Morrell grimaced. "Yes. It makes him sound like a warmhearted liberal, worrying about African-Americans and Indians, when all he really wants to do is keep anyone from inspecting life-insurance records to see how many policies were sold which Illinois insurers don't want to pay out."

"Of course, the Sommers family also bought a policy they can't collect on. Although I don't think it was the company that defrauded them, but the agent. I wish I could see Fepple's file."

"Not today, Ms. Warshawski. I'm not giving back your picklocks until I board that 777 on Tuesday."

I laughed and subsided into the sports section. The Cubs had gone so far into free fall that they'd have to send the space shuttle to haul them back to the National League. The Sox, on the other hand, were looking pretty, the best record in the majors going into the final week of the season. Even though the pundits were saying they'd be eliminated in the first round of the play-offs, it was still an amazing event in Chicago sports.

We reached Orchestra Hall seconds before the ushers closed the doors. Michael Loewenthal had left tickets for Morrell and me. We joined Agnes and Calia Loewenthal in a box, Calia looking angelic in white smocking with gold roses embroidered on it. Her doll and dog, festooned with ribbons in matching gold, were propped up in the chair next to hers.

"Where're Lotty and Max?" I whispered as the musicians took the stage.

"Max is getting ready for the party. Lotty came over to help him, then got into a huge row with both him and Carl. She doesn't look well; I don't know if she'll even stay for the party."

"Shh, Mommy, Aunt Vicory, you can't talk when Daddy is playing in public." Calia looked at us sternly.

She had been warned against this sin many times in her short life. Agnes and I obediently subsided, but my worries about Lotty rushed back to the front of my mind. Also, if she was having a major fight with Max, I wasn't looking forward to the evening.

As the musicians took the stage they looked remote in their formal wear, like strangers, not friends. For a moment I wished we'd skipped the concert, but once the music began, with the controlled lyricism that marked Carl's style, the knots inside me began to unwind. In a Schubert trio, the richness of Michael Loewenthal's playing, and the intimacy he seemed to feel—with his cello, with his fellow musicians—made me ache with longing. Morrell took my fingers and squeezed them gently: separation will not part us.

During intermission, I asked Agnes if she knew why Lotty and Max were fighting.

She shook her head. "Michael says they've been arguing off and on all summer over this conference on Jews where Max spoke on Wednesday. Now they seem to be fighting about a man Max met there, or heard speak, or something, but I was trying to get Calia to hold still while I braided the ribbons into her hair and didn't really pay attention."

After the concert Agnes asked if we would drive Calia up to Evanston with us. "She's been so good, sitting like a princess for three hours. The sooner she can run around and let off steam the better. I'd like to stay until Michael's ready to leave."

Calia's angelic mood vanished as soon as we walked out of Orchestra Hall. She ran shrieking down the street, shedding ribbons and even Ninshubur, the blue stuffed dog. Before she actually careened into the street, I caught up with her and scooped her up.

"I am not a baby, I do not get carried," she yelled at me.

"Of course not. No baby would be such a pain." I was panting with the exertion of carrying her down the stairs to the garage. Morrell was laughing at both of us, which made Calia at once assume an icy dignity.

"I am most annoyed at this behavior," she said, echoing her mother, her little arms crossed in front of her.

"Speaking for both of us," I murmured, setting her back on her feet.

Morrell handed her into the car and gravely offered Ninshubur back to her. Calia wouldn't allow me to fasten her seat belt but decided Morrell was her ally against me and stopped squirming when he leaned in to do the job. On the ride to Max's, she scolded me through the medium of lecturing her doll: "You are a very naughty girl, picking up Ninshubur and carrying him down the stairs when he was running. Ninshubur is not a baby. He needs to run and let off steam." She certainly took my mind off any other worries. Perhaps that would be a good reason to have a child: you wouldn't have energy left to fret about anything else.

A handful of cars were in Max's drive when we got there, including Lotty's dark-green Infiniti, its battered fenders an eloquent testimony to her imperious approach to the streets. She hadn't learned to drive until she arrived in Chicago at the age of thirty, when she apparently took lessons from a NASCAR crash dummy. She must have patched up her disagreement with Max if she was staying for the party.

A black-suited young man opened the door for us. Calia ran down the hall, shrieking for her grandfather. When we moved more slowly after her, we saw two other men in waiters' costumes folding napkins in the dining room. Max had set up a series of small tables there and in the adjacent parlor so that people could eat dinner sitting down.

Lotty, her back to the door, was counting forks into bundles and slapping them onto a sideboard. Judging from her rigid posture she was still angry. We slipped by without saying anything.

"Not the best mood for a party," I muttered.

"We can pay our respects to Carl and leave early," Morrell agreed.

We tracked Max down in the kitchen, where he was conferring with his housekeeper on how to manage the party. Calia ran to tug at his arm. He hoisted her up to the countertop but didn't let her stop his discussion with Mrs. Squires. Max has been an administrator for years—he knows you never finish anything if you keep accepting interruptions.

"What's going on with Lotty?" I asked when he and Mrs. Squires were done.

"Oh, she's having a temper tantrum. I wouldn't pay much attention to it," he said lightly.

"This isn't about the Radbuka business, is it?" I asked, frowning.

"Opa, Opa," Calia shouted, "I was quiet the whole time, but Aunt Vicory and Mommy talked and then Aunt Vicory was very bad, she hurted my tummy when she carried me down the stairs."

"Terrible, *puppchen*," Max murmured, stroking her hair, adding to me, "Lotty and I have agreed to keep our disagreements to one side for the evening. So I am not going to violate the concordat by giving my views."

One of the waiters brought a young woman in jeans into the kitchen. Max introduced her as Lindsey, a local student who was going to entertain the small ones at the party. When I told Calia I'd go upstairs to help her put on play clothes, she told me scornfully it was a *formal* party, so she had to keep her party dress on, but she consented to go with Lindsey to the garden.

Lotty swept into the kitchen, acknowledging Morrell and me with a regal nod, and said she was going up to change. Despite her daunting manner, it was a relief to see her imperious rather than anguished. She reappeared in a crimson silk jacket and long skirt about the time the other guests began to arrive.

Don Strzepek walked over from Morrell's, actually wearing an ironed shirt—Max had readily agreed to include Morrell's old friend in the invitation. The musicians showed up in a bunch. Three or four had children around Calia's age; the cheerful Lindsey scooped them all together and took them upstairs to watch videos and eat pizza.

Carl had changed from his tails into a soft sweater and trousers. His eyes were bright with pleasure in himself, his music, his friends; the tempo of the party began to accelerate with the force of his personality. Even Lotty was relaxing, laughing in one corner with the Cellini bass player.

I found myself discussing Chicago architecture with Michael Loewenthal's first cello instructor. Over wine and little squares of goat-cheese polenta, the Cellini's manager suggested today's anti-American sentiment in France resembled anti-Roman feelings in ancient Gaul. Near the piano Morrell was deep in the kind of political controversy he delights in. We forgot our idea of leaving early.

Around nine, when the rest of the guests had gone into the back of the house for dinner, the doorbell rang. I had lingered in the sunroom, listening to Rosa Ponselle sing *"L'amero, saro costante."* It had been one of my mother's favorite arias and I wanted to hear the recording to the end. The bell rang again as I crossed the empty hall to join the rest of the party—the waiters were apparently too busy serving dinner to respond to it. I turned back to the heavy double doors.

When I saw the figure on the doorstep, I sucked in my breath. His curly hair was thinning at the temples, but despite the grey, and the lines around his mouth, his face had a kind of childlike quality. The pictures I'd been looking at showed him contorted with anguish, but even with his cheeks creased in a shy, eager smile, Paul Radbuka was unmistakable.

XVI

Contact Problems

He looked around the hall with a kind of nervous eagerness, as if he had arrived early for an audition. "Are you Mrs. Loewenthal, perhaps? Or a daughter?"

"Mr. Radbuka—or is it Mr. Ulrich—who invited you here?" I wondered wildly if that was what Lotty and Max had been fighting about—Max had found the guy's address and invited him to come while Carl was still in town; Lotty, with her intense fear of reawakening the past, strenuously objected.

"No, no, Ulrich was never my name; that was the man who called himself my father. I'm Paul Radbuka. Are you one of my new relatives?"

"Why are you here? Who invited you?" I repeated.

"No one. I came on my own, when Rhea told me that some of the people who knew my family, or perhaps are my family, were leaving Chicago tomorrow."

"When I talked to Rhea Wiell Friday afternoon, she said you didn't know there were any other Radbukas and that she'd see how you felt about meeting them."

"Oh. Oh—you were part of that meeting with Rhea. Are you the publisher who wants to write my story?"

"I'm V I Warshawski. I'm an investigator who spoke to her about the possibility of meeting you." I knew I sounded chilly, but his unexpected arrival had me off-balance.

"I know—the detective who went to see her when she was talking to her publisher. Then you're the person who is friends with the survivors from my family."

"No," I said sharply, trying to slow him down. "I have friends who may know someone from the Radbuka family. Whether that person is related to you would depend on a lot of details that we can't really get into tonight. Why don't you—"

He interrupted me, his eager smile replaced by anger. "I want to meet anyone who could possibly be a relative. Not in some cautious way, going back to you, finding out who these other Radbukas are, checking to see whether they could really be related to me, whether they want to meet me. That might take months, even years—I can't wait for that kind of time to pass."

"So you prayed and the Lord directed you to Mr. Loewenthal's address?" I said.

Spots of color burned in his cheeks. "You're being sarcastic, but there's no need to be. I learned at Rhea's that Max Loewenthal was the man who was interested in finding me. That he had a musician friend who knew my family, and that the musician was here only until tomorrow. When she put it like that, that Max and his friend thought they might know someone of my family, I knew the truth: either Max or his musician friend must be my missing relation. They are hiding behind a cloak of pretending to have a friend—I know that—it's a common disguise, especially for people who are frightened of having their identities known. I saw I would have to take the initiative, come to them, overcome their fears of being found out. So I studied the newspapers, I saw the Cellini was visiting from England, with their last concert today, I saw the name *Loewenthal* as the cellist and knew he must be Max's relation."

"Rhea told you Mr. Loewenthal's name?" I demanded, furious with her for breaching Max's privacy.

He gave a supercilious smile. "She made it clear she wanted me to learn it: she'd written Max's name next to mine in her appointment book. Which made me sure Max and I were linked."

I remembered reading her square hand upside down myself. I felt overwhelmed by his easy manipulation of facts to suit his wishes and demanded sharply how he'd found Max's house, since his home phone isn't listed.

"Oh, it was simple." He laughed with childish delight, his anger forgotten. "I told them at the symphony I was Michael Loewenthal's cousin and that I badly needed to see him while he was still in town."

"And the CSO gave you this address?" I was staggered: stalking is such a serious problem for performers that no symphony management worth its salt gives out home addresses.

"No, no." He laughed again. "If you're a detective, this will amuse you, maybe even be useful to you in your work. I did try to get the address from the symphony management, but they were very stuffy. So today I went to the concert. What a beautiful gift Michael has—how wonderfully he plays on that cello. I went backstage afterward to congratulate him, but that wasn't so easy, either—they make it hard to get in to see the performers."

He scowled in momentary resentment. "By the time I got backstage, my cousin Michael had left, but I heard the other performers talking about the party that Max was holding tonight. So I called the hospital where Max works and told them I was with the chamber players but I had lost Max's address. So they found someone in the administration—it took a while, because it's Sunday, that's why I'm late—but they called me with the address."

"How did you know where Mr. Loewenthal works?" I was reeling so hard in the face of his narrative that I could only grasp at the corner points.

"It was in the program, the program for the Birnbaum conference." He beamed with pride. "Wasn't that clever, to say I was one of the musicians? Isn't that the kind of thing an investigator like you does to find people?"

It made me furious that he was right—it's exactly what I would have done. "Despite how clever it was, you're here under a false impression. Max Loewenthal is not your cousin."

He smiled indulgently. "Yes, yes, I'm sure you're protecting him—Rhea told me you were protecting him and that she respected you for it, but consider this: he wants to find out about me. What other possible reason could there be than that he knows we're related?"

We were still standing in the doorway. "You yourself know there's a party going on. Mr. Loewenthal can't possibly give you proper attention tonight. Why don't you give me your address and phone number—he will want to meet you when he can give you his total attention. You should go home before you find yourself in the embarrassing predicament of trying to explain yourself to a room full of strangers."

"You're not Max's daughter or his wife, you're only a guest here as I am myself," Radbuka snapped. "I want to meet him while his son and his friend are still here. Which one is his friend? There were three men of the right age playing in the concert."

Out of the corner of my eye, I saw a couple of people drifting back from the dining room toward the front of the house. I took Radbuka, or Ulrich, or whoever he was, by the elbow. "Why don't we go out to a coffee shop, where we can talk this over privately. Then we can figure out whether there's any chance you could be related to—anyone in Mr. Loewenthal's milieu. But this public forum isn't the best way to do it."

He wrenched himself away. "How do you spend your time? Looking for people's missing jewelry or their lost dogs? You're a property investigator. But I am not a piece of property, I am a man. After all these years—all these deaths and separations—to think I might have some family that survived the Shoah, I don't want to waste one more second before seeing them, let alone one more week or years, even, while you file information about me." His voice thickened with feeling.

"I thought—in your television interview last week, you said you'd only recently discovered your past?"

"But it's been weighing on me all this time, even though I didn't know it. You don't know what it was like, to grow up with a monster, a sadist, and never understand the reason for his hatred: he had attached himself to someone he despised in order to get a visa to America. If I had known what he really was—what he had done in Europe—I would have had him deported. Now, to have the chance to meet my true family—I will not let you put any barriers in my path." Tears started down his face.

"Even so, if you leave your details with me, I will see that Mr. Loewenthal gets them. He will arrange an appointment with you at an early date, but this—confronting him in a public gathering— what kind of welcome do you think he would give you?" I tried to hide my anxiety and dismay under a copy of Rhea Wiell's saintly smile.

"The same welcome I will give him—the heartfelt embrace of one survivor of the ashes to another. There is no way you can understand that."

"Understand what?" Max himself suddenly appeared with the Cellini oboist on his arm. "Victoria, is this a guest whom I should know?"

"Are you Max?" Radbuka pushed past me to Max, grasping his hand, his face shining with pleasure. "Oh, that I had words to express how much this night means to me. To be able to greet my true cousin. Max. Max."

Max looked from Radbuka to me with the same confusion I was feeling. "I'm sorry, I don't know—oh—you—are you—Victoria—is this your doing?"

"No, it was all mine," Radbuka crowed in delight. "Victoria had mentioned your name to Rhea, and I knew you must be my cousin, either you or your friend. Why else would Victoria be trying so hard to protect you?"

Radbuka adapted himself quickly to the environment: he hadn't known my name when he arrived; now I was Victoria. He also made the childlike assumption that the people in his special world, like Rhea, must be familiar to anyone he spoke to.

"But why discuss me with this therapist at all?" Max said.

The crowd growing behind him included Don Strzepek, who stepped forward. "I'm afraid that was my doing, Mr. Loewenthal— I mentioned your first name, and Rhea Wiell immediately guessed it was you because you'd been on the program at the Birnbaum conference."

I made a helpless gesture. "I've tried to suggest to Mr.— Radbuka—that he come away with me to talk over his situation quietly."

"An excellent idea. Why don't you let Ms. Warshawski get you some supper, and go up to my study where I might be able to join you in an hour or so." Max was off-balance but trying to handle the situation gracefully.

Paul laughed, bobbing his head up and down. "I know, I know. Rhea suggested you might be reluctant to be public with our relationship. But truly, you have nothing to fear—I am not planning on asking for money, or anything of that nature—the man who called himself my father left me well off. Although since the money came from acts of monstrosity, perhaps I should not be taking it. But if he couldn't care for me emotionally, at least he tried to compensate with money."

"You came to my house under false pretenses. I assure you, Mr. Radbuka: I am not related to the Radbuka family."

"Are you ashamed?" Paul blurted. "But I'm not here to embarrass you, only to finally find my family, to see what I can learn about my past, my life before Terezin."

"What little I know I will tell you another time. When I'm at leisure to attend to you properly." Max took his elbow, trying futilely to propel him to the door. "And what you know about yourself you can tell me. Give your phone number to Ms. Warshawski and I will get in touch with you. Tomorrow, I promise you."

Radbuka's face crumpled, like a child about to cry. He reiterated his speech about not being able to wait one more minute. "And tomorrow your musician friend will be gone. What if he's the one who is my missing cousin—how will I ever find him again?"

"Don't you see," Max began helplessly. "All this flailing around with no information is only harder on you, harder on me. Please. Let Ms. Warshawski take you upstairs and talk to you in a quiet way. Or leave your number with her and go home now."

"But I came here by taxi. I can't drive. I don't have a way home," Radbuka cried out in a childlike bewilderment. "Why won't you make me welcome?"

As more people finished dinner, they began filling the hall on their way to the front room. An altercation at the foot of the stairs was a lightning rod for attention. The crowd began to grow, pressing against Max.

I took Paul's arm again. "You are welcome—but not arguing in the hall in the middle of a party. Rhea wouldn't want you to be so distressed, would she? Let's sit down where we can be comfortable."

"Not until I meet Max's musician friend," he said stubbornly. "Not until he tells me to my face that he knows me, remembers the mother whom I saw pushed alive into a pit of lime."

Lotty had appeared at the door connecting the living room to the hall. She pushed her way through the group to my side. "What's going on, Victoria?"

"This is the guy calling himself Radbuka," I muttered to her. "He got here through some unfortunate fast footwork on his part."

Behind us, we heard a woman echo Lotty's question to someone else in the crowd. And we also heard the response: "I'm not sure; I think this man may be claiming Carl Tisov is his father or something."

Radbuka heard her as well. "Carl Tisov? Is that the name of the musician? Is he here now?"

Lotty's eyes widened in dismay. I whirled, determined to deny the rumor before it got started, but the crowd surged forward, the buzz catching like fire on straw and spreading through the room. Carl's appearance at the back of the hall caused a sudden silence.

"What is this?" he asked gaily. "Are you having a prayer vigil out here, Loewenthal?"

"Is that Carl?" Paul's face lit up again. "Is it you who is my cousin? Oh, Carl, I am here, your long-lost relation. Perhaps we are even brothers? Oh, will you people please move out of the way? I need to get to him!"

"This is horrifying," Lotty muttered in my ear. "How did he get here? How did he decide Carl was related to him?"

The crowd stood frozen with the embarrassment people get when confronted with an adult whose emotions are running wild. As Paul tried to push his way through the throng, Calia suddenly appeared at the top of the hall, shrieking loudly. The other small ones followed, yelling just as loudly, as she pelted down the stairs. Lindsey was running after them, trying to reestablish order—some game must have gotten out of hand.

Calia stopped on the lower landing when she realized the size of her audience. Then she gave a loud whoop of laughter and pointed at Paul. "Look, it's the big bad wolf, he's going to eat my grandpa. He'll catch us next."

All the children took up the chant, pointing at Paul and screeching, "It's a wolf, it's a wolf, it's the big bad wolf!"

When Paul realized he was the object of their taunting, he started to tremble. I thought he might cry again.

Agnes Loewenthal elbowed her way through the packed hall. She stomped up the short flight to the lower landing and scooped up her daughter.

"You're over the top just now, young lady. You littlies were supposed to stay in the playroom with Lindsey: I'm most annoyed at this behavior. It's long past time for your bath and bed—you've had enough excitement for the day."

Calia began to howl, but Agnes marched up to the upper landing with her. The other children became quiet at once. They tiptoed up the stairs in front of a red-faced Lindsey.

The lesser drama with the children had unfrozen the crowd. They let Michael Loewenthal divert them into the front room where coffee was set up. I saw Morrell, who had appeared in the hall when my attention was on Calia, talking to Max and Don.

Radbuka was covering his face in distress. "Why is everyone treating me this way? The wolf, the big bad wolf, that was my foster father. Ulrich, that's German for wolf, but it isn't my name. Who told the children to call me that?"

"No one," I said crisply, my sympathy worn completely thin. "The children were acting out, the way children will. No one here knows that Ulrich is German for big bad wolf."

"It isn't." I'd forgotten Lotty was standing behind me. "It's one of those medieval totemic names, wolflike ruler, something like that." She added something in German to Paul.

Paul started to answer her in German, then stuck out his lower lip, like Calia's when she was being stubborn. "I will not speak the language of my slavery. Are you German? Did you know the man who called himself my father?"

Lotty sighed. "I'm American. But I speak German."

Paul's mood shifted upward again; he beamed at Lotty. "But you are a friend of Max and Carl's. So I was right to come here. If you know my family, did you know Sofie Radbuka?"

At that question, Carl turned to stare at him. "Where the hell did you come up with that name? Lotty, what do you know about this? Did you bring this man here to taunt Max and me?"

"I?" Lotty said. "I—need to sit down."

Her face had gone completely white. I was just in time to catch her as her knees buckled.

XVII

Digging Up the Past

Morrell helped me support Lotty into the sunroom, where we laid her on a wicker settee. She hadn't fainted completely but was still pale and glad to lie down. Max, his face pinched with worry, covered Lotty with an afghan. Always calm in a crisis, he sent Don to the housekeeper for a bottle of ammonia. When I'd soaked a napkin with it and waved it under her nose, Lotty's color improved. She pushed herself to a sitting position, urging Max to return to his guests. After assuring himself that she was really better, he reluctantly went back to the party.

"Melodrama must be in the air this evening," Lotty said, trying unsuccessfully for her usual manner. "I've never done that before in my life. Who brought that extraordinary man here? Surely that wasn't you, Victoria?"

"He brought himself," I said. "He has an eel-like ability to wiggle into spaces. Including the hospital, where some moron in admin gave him Max's home address."

Morrell coughed warningly, jerking his head at the shadows on the far side of the room. Paul Radbuka was standing there, just beyond the edge of the circle of light cast by a floor lamp. Now he darted forward to stand over Lotty.

"Are you feeling better now? Do you feel like talking? I think you must know Sofie Radbuka. Who is she? How can I find her? She must be related to me in some way."

"Surely the person you are looking for was named Miriam." Despite her shaking hands, Lotty pulled herself together to use her "Princess of Austria" manner.

"My Miriam, yes, I long to find her again. But Sofie Radbuka, that is a name which was dangled in front of me like a carrot, making me believe one of my relations must still be alive somewhere. Only now the carrot has been withdrawn. But I'm sure you know her, why else did you faint when you heard the name?"

A question whose answer I would have liked to hear myself, but not in front of this guy.

Lotty raised haughty eyebrows at him. "What I do is no conceivable business of yours. It was my understanding from the uproar you caused in the hall that you came to see whether either Mr. Loewenthal or Mr. Tisov were related to you. Now that you've caused a great disturbance, perhaps you would be good enough to give your address to Ms. Warshawski and leave us in peace."

Radbuka's lower lip stuck out, but before he could dig his heels in, Morrell intervened. "I'm going to take Radbuka up to Max's study, as V I tried to do an hour ago. Max and Carl may join him there later, if they're able."

Don had been sitting quietly in the background, but he stood up now. "Right. Come on, big guy. Dr. Herschel needs to rest."

Don put an arm around him. With Morrell at his other elbow, they moved the unhappy Radbuka to the door, his neck hunched into his oversize jacket, his face so expressive of bewildered misery that he looked like a circus clown.

When they'd gone, I turned to Lotty. "Who was Sofie Radbuka?"

She turned her frosty stare to me. "No one that I know of."

"Then why did hearing her name make you faint?"

"It didn't. My foot caught on the edge of a rug and—"

"Lotty, if you don't want to tell me, keep it to yourself, but please don't make up stupid lies to me."

She bit her lip, turning her head away from me. "There's been far too much emotion in this house today. First Max and Carl furious with me, and now the man himself shows up. I don't need you angry with me as well."

I sat on the wicker table in front of her settee. "I'm not angry. But I happened to be alone in the hall when this guy came to the door, and after ten minutes with him my head was spinning like a hula hoop. If you faint, or start to faint, then claim nothing was wrong, it makes me even dizzier. I'm not here to criticize, but you were so upset on Friday you got me seriously worried. And your agony seems to have started with this guy's appearance at the Birnbaum conference."

She looked back at me, her hauteur suddenly changed to consternation. "Victoria, I'm sorry—I have been selfish, not thinking of the effect of my behavior on you. You do deserve some kind of explanation."

She sat frowning to herself, as if trying to decide what kind of explanation I deserved. "I don't know if I can make clear the relationships of that time in my life. How I came to be so close to Max, and even Carl.

"There was a group of nine of us refugee children who became good friends during the war. We met over music; a woman from Salzburg, a violist who was herself a refugee, came around London and gathered us up. She saw Carl's gift, got him lessons, got him into a good music program. There were various others. Teresz, who eventually married Max. Me. My father had been a violin player. Café music, not the stuff of the soirées Frau Herbst organized, but skillful—at least, I think he was skillful, but how can I know, when I only heard him as a child? Anyway, even though I had no gift myself, I loved hearing the music at Frau Herbst's."

"Was Radbuka the name of one of that group? Why does Carl care so much? Is it someone he was in love with?"

She smiled painfully. "You would have to ask him that. Radbuka was the name of—someone else. Max—he had great organizational skills, even as a young man. When the war ended, he went around London to the different societies that helped people find out about their families. Then he—went back to central Europe, looking. That was in—I think it was in '47, but after all this time I can't be sure of the exact year. That was when the Radbuka name came up—it wasn't anyone in the group's actual surname, you see. But that is why we could ask Max to look. Because we were all so close, not like a family, like something else, perhaps a combat team who fought together for years.

"For almost all of us, Max's reports came back with devastating completeness. No survivors. For the Herschels, the Tisovs, the Loewenthals—Max found his father and two cousins, and that was another terrible—" She cut herself off mid-sentence.

"I was starting my medical training. It consumed me to the exclusion of so much else. Carl always blamed me for—well, let's just say, something unpleasant came up around the person from the Radbuka family. Carl always thought my absorption with medicine made me behave in a fashion which he regarded as cruel . . . as if his own devotion to music had not been equally absolute."

This last sentence she muttered under her breath as an after-thought. She fell silent. She had never spoken to me of her losses in such a way, such an emotional way. I didn't understand what she was trying to say—or not to say—about the friend from the Radbuka family, but when it became clear she wouldn't expand on it, I couldn't press her.

"Do you know"—I hesitated, trying to think of the least painful way of asking the question—"do you know what Max learned about the Radbuka family?"

Her face twisted. "They—he didn't find any trace of them. Although traces were hard to find and he didn't have much money. We all gave him a bit, but we didn't have money, either."

"So hearing this man call himself Radbuka must have been quite a shock."

She shuddered and looked at me. "It was, believe me, it's been a shock all week. How I envy Carl, able to put the whole world to one side when he starts to play. Or maybe it's that he puts the whole world inside him and blows it out that tube." She repeated the question she'd asked when she saw Paul on video. "How old is he, do you think?"

"He says he came here after the war around the age of four, so he must have been born in '42 or '43."

"So he couldn't be—does he think he was born in Theresienstadt?"

I threw up my hands. "All I know about him is from Wednesday night's interview. Is Theresienstadt the same as what he calls Terezin?"

"Terezin is its Czech name; it's an old fortress outside Prague." She added with an unexpected gleam of humor, "That's Austrian snobbery, using the German name—a holdover from when Prague was part of the Hapsburg empire and everyone spoke German. This man tonight, he's insisting he's Czech, not German, by calling it Terezin."

We sat again in silence. Lotty was withdrawn into her own thoughts, but she seemed more relaxed, less tortured, than she had for the past few days. I told her I'd go up to see what I could learn from Radbuka.

Lotty nodded. "If I feel stronger I'll come up by and by. Right now—I think I'll just lie here."

I made sure she was well-covered in the afghan Max had pro-vided before turning out the light. When I closed the French doors behind me, I could see across the hall into the front room, where a dozen or so people still lingered over brandy. Michael Loewenthal was on the piano bench, holding Agnes on his lap. Everyone was happy. I went on up the stairs.

Max's study was a large room overlooking the lake, filled with Ming vases and T'ang horses. It was at the far end of the second floor from where the children were watching videos; Max had picked the room when his own two children were small, because it was well-secluded from the body of the house. When I shut the door no outside sounds could disrupt the tension inside. Morrell and Don smiled at me, but Paul Ulrich-Radbuka looked away in disappointment when he saw it was me, not Max or Carl.

"I don't understand what's happening," he said pathetically. "Are people ashamed to be seen with me? I need to talk to Max and Carl. I need to find out how we're related. I'm sure Carl or Max will want to know he has a surviving family member."

I squeezed my eyes shut, as if that would block out his hyper-emotional state. "Try to relax, Mr.—uh. Mr. Loewenthal will be with you as soon as he can leave his guests. Perhaps Mr. Tisov as well. Can I get you a glass of wine, or a soft drink?"

He looked longingly at the door but apparently realized he couldn't find Carl unaided. He subsided into an armchair and muttered that he supposed a glass of water would help settle his nerves. Don jumped up to fetch it.

I decided the only way to get any information out of him would be to act as though I believed in his identity. He was so unstable, leaping up the scale from misery to ecstasy by octaves, weaving straws in the conversation into clothes, that I wasn't sure anything he said would be reliable, but if I challenged him, he would only retreat into a defensive weeping.

"Do you have any clue about where you were born?" I asked. "I gather Radbuka is a Czech name."

"The birth certificate that was sent with me to Terezin said Berlin, which is one reason I'm so eager to meet my relatives. Maybe the Radbukas were Czechs hiding in Berlin: some Jews fled west instead of east, trying to get away from the *Einsatzgruppen*. Maybe they were Czechs who had emigrated there before the war ever started. Oh, how I wish I knew something." He knotted his hands in anguish.

I picked my next words with care. "It must have been quite a shock to you, to find that birth certificate when your—uh—foster father died. Telling you that you were Paul Radbuka from Berlin, instead of—where did Ulrich tell you you were born?"

"Vienna. But no, I've never seen my Terezin birth certificate, I only read about it elsewhere, once I realized who I was."

"How cruel of Ulrich, to write about it but not leave you with the document itself!" I exclaimed.

"No, no, I had to track it down in an outside report. It was—was just by chance I found out about it at all."

"What an extraordinary amount of research you've done!" I packed my voice with so much admiration that Morrell frowned at me in warning, but Paul brightened perceptibly. "I'd love to see the report that told you about your birth certificate."

At that he stiffened, so I hastily changed the subject. "You don't remember any Czech, I suppose, if you were separated from your mother at—what was it—twelve months?"

He relaxed again. "When I hear Czech I recognize it but don't really understand it. The first language I spoke is German, because that was the language of the guards. Also many of the women who worked in the nursery at Terezin spoke it."

I heard the door open behind me and held a hand out in a signal to be quiet. Don slid past me to put a glass of water next to Paul. Out of the corner of my eye I saw Max quietly follow Don into the room. Paul, caught up in the pleasure of my attending to his story, went on without paying attention to them.

"There were six of us small children who more or less banded together, and really, we formed a little brigade; even at the age of three we looked after one another because the adults were so overworked and so underfed they couldn't care for individual children. We clung to one another and hid together from the guards. When the war ended we were sent to England. At first we were scared when the adults started putting us on trains, because in Terezin we saw many children put on trains and everyone knew they went someplace to die. But after we got over our terror, we had a happy time in England. We were in a big house in the country, it had a name like that of an animal, a dog, which was scary at first because we were terrified of dogs. From having seen them used so evilly in the camps."

"And that's where you learned English?" I prompted.

"We learned English bit by bit, the way children do, and really, we forgot our German. After a time, maybe it was nine months or even a year, they started finding homes for us, people wanting to adopt us. They decided we were mentally recovered enough that we could stand the pain of losing one another, although how can you ever stand that pain? The loss of my special playmate, my Miriam, it haunts my dreams to this day."

His voice broke. He used the napkin Don had put under the water glass to blow his nose. "One day this man arrived. He was large and coarse-faced and said he was my father and I should go with him. He wouldn't even let me kiss my little Miriam good-bye. Kissing was *weibisch*—a sissy thing—and I must be a man now. He shouted to me in German and was furious that I didn't speak German anymore. Over and over as I was growing up he would beat me, telling me he was making a man out of me, beating the *Schwul und Weiblichkeit* out of me."

He was crying freely, in obvious distress. I handed him the glass of water.

"That must have been very horrible," Max said gravely. "When did your father die?"

He didn't seem to notice Max's sudden appearance in the conversation. "You mean, I presume, the man who is *not* my father. I don't know when my birth father died. That is what I am hoping you can tell me. Or perhaps Carl Tisov."

He blew his nose again and stared at us defiantly. "The man who stole me from my campmates died seven years ago. It was after that when I started having nightmares and became depressed and disoriented. I lost my job, I lost my bearings, my nightmares became more and more explicit. I tried various remedies, but—always I was being drawn to these unspeakable images of the past, images I have come to recognize as my experience of the Shoah. Not until I started working with Rhea did I understand them for what they were. I think I saw my mother being raped and pushed alive into a pit of lime, but of course it could have been some other woman, I was so little I can't even recall my mother's face."

"Did your foster father tell you what became of—well, his wife?" Morrell put in.

"He said the woman he called my mother had died when the Allies bombed Vienna. That we had lived in Vienna and lost everything because of the Jews, he was always very bitter about the Jews."

"Do you have any idea why he tracked you down in England? Or how he knew you were there?" I was struggling to make sense of his narrative.

He spread his hands in a gesture of bewilderment. "After the war—everything was so unsettled. Anything was possible. I think he wanted to come to America, and claiming he was a Jew, which he could do if he had a Jewish child in hand, that would put him at the head of the queue. Especially if he had a Nazi past he wanted to conceal."

"And you think he did?" Max asked.

"I know so. I know so from his papers, that he was a vile piece of *drek*. A leader of the *Einsatzgruppen*."

"What a horrible thing to uncover," Don murmured. "To be a Jew and find you've grown up with the worst of the murderers of your people. No wonder he treated you the way he did."

Paul looked at him eagerly. "Oh, you do understand! I'm sure that his bestial behavior—the way he would beat me, deprive me of food when he was angry, lock me in a closet for hours, sometimes overnight—all that came from his terrible anti-Semitism. You are a Jew, Mr. Loewenthal, you understand how ugly someone like that can be."

Max sidestepped the remark. "Ms. Warshawski says that you found a document in your—foster father's—papers that gave you the clue to your real name. I'm curious about that. Would you let me see it?"

Ulrich-Radbuka took his time to answer. "When you tell me which one of you is related to me, then perhaps I will let you see the papers. But since you will not help me, I see no reason why I should show you my private documents."

"Neither Mr. Tisov nor I is connected to the Radbuka family," Max said. "Please try to accept that. It is a different friend of ours who knew a family with your name, but I know as much as that person does about the Radbuka family—which I'm sorry to say isn't a great deal. If you could let me see these documents, it would help me decide if you are part of the same family."

When Radbuka refused in a panicky voice, I intervened to ask if he had any idea where his birth parents came from. Apparently taking the question as agreement to his Radbuka identity, Paul recounted what he knew with a return of his childlike eagerness.

"I know nothing whatsoever about my birth parents. Some of our six musketeers knew more, although that can be painful, too. My little Miriam, for instance, poor soul, she knew her mother had gone mad and died in the mental hospital at Terezin. But now—Max, you say you know the details of my family life. Who of the Radbukas would be in Berlin in 1942?"

"No one," Max said with finality. "No brothers, nor parents. I can assure you of that. This is a family which emigrated to Vienna in the years before the First World War. In 1941 they were sent to Lodz, in Poland. The ones who were still alive in 1943 were sent on to the camp where they all perished."

Paul Ulrich-Radbuka's face lit up. "But perhaps I was born in Lodz."

"I thought you knew you'd been born in Berlin," I blurted out.

"There are so few reliable documents from those times," he said. "Perhaps they gave me the paper of a boy who died in the camp. Anything like that is possible."

Talking to him was like walking in the marshes: just when you thought you had a fact to stand on, the ground gave way.

Max looked at him gravely. "None of the Radbukas in Vienna had special standing: they weren't important socially or artistically, as was typically true of people who were sent to Theresien—to Terezin. Of course there were always exceptions, but I doubt you will find them in this case."

"So you're trying to tell me my family doesn't exist. But I can see it's just that you're hiding them from me. I demand to see them in person. I know they will claim me when they meet me."

"One easy solution to the problem is a DNA test," I suggested. "Max, Carl, and their English friend could give blood, we could agree on a lab in England or the U.S. and send a sample of Mr.—Mr. Radbuka's blood there, as well. That would resolve the question of whether he's related to any of you or to Max's English friend."

"I am not uncertain!" Paul exclaimed, his face pink. "You may be; you're a detective who makes a living by being suspicious. But I will not submit to being treated like a laboratory specimen, the way my people were in that medical laboratory at Auschwitz, the way my little Miriam's mother was treated. Looking at blood samples is what the Nazis cared about. Heredity, race, all those things, I won't take part in it."

"That brings us back to where we started," I said. "With a document that you alone know about and no way for suspicious detectives like me to verify your certainty. By the way, who is Sofie Radbuka?"

Paul turned sulky. "She was on the Web. Someone in a missing-persons chat room said they wanted information about a Sofie Radbuka who lived in England in the forties. So I wrote saying she must be my mother, and the person never wrote back."

"Right now we're all exhausted," Max said. "Mr. Radbuka, why don't you write down everything you know about your family? I will get my friend to do the same. You can give me your document and I will give you the other one. Then we can meet again to compare notes."

Radbuka sat with his lower lip sticking out, not even looking up to acknowledge the suggestion. When Morrell, with a grimace at the clock, said he'd drive him home, Radbuka refused at first to get up.

Max looked at him sternly. "You must leave now, Mr. Radbuka, unless you wish to create a situation in which you would never be able to return here."

His clown face a tragic mask, Radbuka got to his feet. With Morrell and Don again at his elbows, like wardens in a high-class mental hospital, he shambled sullenly to the door.

XVIII

Old Lovers

Downstairs, the party was over. The waitstaff was cleaning up the remains, vacuuming food from the carpets and washing up the last of the dishes. In the living room, Carl and Michael were debating the tempo in a Brahms nonet, playing passages on the grand piano while Agnes Loewenthal watched from a couch with her legs curled under her.

She looked up when I glanced in the doorway, hurriedly untangling her feet to run over to me before I could follow Morrell and Don outside. "Vic! Who is that extraordinary man? Carl has been beside himself over this intrusion. He went into the sunroom and shouted at Lotty about it until Michael stopped him. What is going on?"

I shook my head. "I honestly don't know. This guy thinks he spent his childhood in the camps. He says he only recently discovered his birth name was Radbuka, so he came here hoping Max or Carl was related to him, because he thought that one of their friends in England had family of that name."

"But that doesn't make sense!" Agnes cried.

Max came down the stairs behind us, his gait heavy with extreme weariness. "So he's gone, is he, Victoria? No, it doesn't make sense. Nothing tonight made much sense. Lotty fainting? I've watched her take bullets out of people without flinching. What did you think of this creature, Victoria? Do you believe his story? It's an extraordinary tale."

I was so tired myself that I was seeing sparks in front of my eyes. "I don't know what I think. He's so volatile, moving from tears to triumphal glee and back in thirty seconds. And every time he gets a new piece of information, he changes his story. Where was he born? In Lodz? Berlin? Vienna? I'm staggered that Rhea Wiell would hypnotize someone that unstable—I'd think it would demolish his fragile connection to reality. But—all these symptoms *could* be caused by exactly what he says happened to him. An infancy spent in Terezin—I don't know how you'd recover from that."

In the living room, Michael and Carl were playing the same passage on the piano over and over, with variations in tempo and tone that were too subtle for me. The repetition began grating on me.

The door to the sunroom opened and Lotty came into the hall, pale but composed. "Sorry, Max," she murmured. "Sorry to leave you alone to deal with him, but I couldn't face him. Nor could Carl, apparently—he came in to castigate me for refusing to join you upstairs. Now I gather Carl has returned to the world of music, leaving this one in our possession."

"Lotty." Max held up a hand. "If you and Carl want to keep fighting, take it someplace else. Neither of you had anything to contribute to what was going on upstairs. But one thing I would like to know—"

The doorbell interrupted him—Morrell, returning with Don.

"He must live close by," I said. "You were hardly gone a minute."

Morrell came over to me. "He asked to be dropped at a place where he could get a cab. Which frankly I was happy to do. A little of the guy goes far with me, so I left him in front of the Orrington, where there's a taxi stand."

"Did you get his address?"

Morrell shook his head. "I asked when we got into the car, but he announced he would go home by cab."

"I tried asking for it, too," Don said, "because of course I want to interview him, but he'd decided we were an untrustworthy bunch."

"Ah, nuts," I said. "Now I'm back to square one with finding him. Unless I can track the cab."

"Did he say anything upstairs?" Lotty asked. "Anything about how he came to think his name was Radbuka?"

I leaned against Morrell, swaying with fatigue. "Just more mumbo jumbo about these mystery documents of his father. Foster father. And how they proved Ulrich was part of the *Einsatzgruppen*."

"What's that?" Agnes asked, her blue eyes troubled.

"Special forces that committed special atrocities in eastern Europe during the war," Max said tersely. "Lotty, since you're feeling better, I would like some information from you now: who is Sofie Radbuka? I think you might explain to me, and to Vic here, why it had such an effect on you."

"I told Vic," Lotty said. "I told her the Radbukas were one of the families that you inquired about for our group of friends in London."

I'd been about to suggest to Morrell that we go home, but I wanted to hear what Lotty would say to Max. "Could we sit down?" I asked Max. "I'm dead on my feet."

"Victoria, of course." Max ushered us into the living room, where Carl and Michael were still fiddling with their music.

Michael looked over at us. He told Carl they could finish the discussion on the way to Los Angeles and came over to sit next to Agnes. I pictured Michael with his cello stuck between his legs in an airplane seat, bowing the same twelve measures over and over while Carl played them on his clarinet at a different pace.

"You haven't eaten, have you?" Morrell said to me. "Let me try to rustle you up a snack—you'll feel better."

"You didn't get dinner?" Max exclaimed. "All this upheaval is erasing ordinary courtesy from my mind."

He sent one of the waiters to the kitchen for a tray of leftovers and drinks. "Now, Lotty, it's your turn on the hot seat. I've respected your privacy all these years and I will continue to do so. But you need to explain to us why the name Sofie Radbuka rattled you so badly this evening. I know I looked for Radbukas for you in Vienna after the war. Who were they?"

"It wasn't the name," Lotty said. "It was the whole aspect of that—" She broke off, biting her lip like a schoolgirl, when she saw Max gravely shake his head.

"It—it was someone at the hospital," Lotty muttered, looking at the carpet. "At the Royal Free. Who didn't want their name public."

"So that was it," Carl said with a venom that startled all of us. "I knew it at the time. I knew it and you denied it."

Lotty flushed, a wave of crimson almost as dark as her jacket. "You made such stupid accusations that I didn't think you deserved an answer."

"About what?" Agnes asked, as bewildered as I was.

Carl said, "You must have realized by now that Lotty and I were lovers for some years in London. I thought it would be forever, but that's because I didn't know Lotty had married medicine."

"Unlike you and music," Lotty snapped.

"Right," I said, leaning over to serve myself scalloped potatoes and salmon from the tray the waiter had brought. "You both had strong senses of vocation. Neither of you would budge. Then what happened?"

"Then Lotty developed TB. Or so she said." Carl bit off the words.

He turned back to Lotty. "You never told me you were ill. You never said good-bye! I got your letter—letter? A notice in *The Times* would have told me more!—when I returned from Edinburgh, there it was, that cold, cryptic note. I ran across town. That imbecile landlady in your lodgings—I can still see her face, with the horrible mole on her nose and all the hairs sticking out of it—she told me. She was smirking. From *her* I learned you were in the country. From *her* I learned you'd instructed her to forward all your mail to Claire Tallmadge, the Ice Queen. Not from you. I loved you. I thought you loved me. But you couldn't even tell me good-bye."

He stopped, panting, then added bitterly, "To this day I do not understand why you let that Tallmadge woman run you around the way she did," he said to Lotty. "She was so—so supercilious. You were her little Jewish pet. Couldn't you ever see how she looked down on you? And the rest of that family. The vapid sister, Vanessa, and her insufferable husband, what was his name? Marmalade?"

"Marmaduke," Lotty said. "As you know quite well, Carl. Besides, you resented anyone I paid more attention to than you."

"My God, you two," Max said. "You should join Calia up in the nursery. Could we get to the point?"

"Besides," Lotty said, flushing again at Max's criticism, "when I returned to the Royal Free, Claire—Claire felt her friendship with me was inappropriate. She—I didn't even know she retired until I saw it in the Royal Free newsletter this spring."

"What did the Radbukas have to do with this?" Don asked.

"I went to see Queen Claire," Carl snarled. "She told me she was forwarding Lotty's mail to a receiving office in Axmouth in care of someone named Sofie Radbuka. But when I wrote, my mail was returned to me, with a note scribbled on the envelope that there was no one there by that name. I even took a train out from London one Monday and walked three miles through the countryside to this cottage. There were lights on inside, Lotty, but you wouldn't answer the door. I stayed there all afternoon, but you never came out.